MOLLY IN THE MIDDLE

IN THE

Also by Ronni Arno

Ruby Reinvented

Dear Poppy

Best. Night. Ever.
(with coauthors)

MOLLY IN THE MIDDLE

Ronni Arno

m!x
aladdin

ALADDIN M!X
New York London Toronto Sydney New Delhi

This book is a work of fiction. Any references to historical events, real people, or real places are used fictitiously. Other names, characters, places, and events are products of the author's imagination, and any resemblance to actual events or places or persons, living or dead, is entirely coincidental.

ALADDIN M!X

Simon & Schuster Children's Publishing Division

1230 Avenue of the Americas, New York, New York 10020

First Aladdin M!X edition October 2017

Text copyright © 2017 by Ronni Arno Blaisdell

Cover illustration copyright © 2017 by Ashleigh Beevers

Also available in an Aladdin hardcover edition.

All rights reserved, including the right of reproduction in whole or in part in any form.

ALADDIN and related logo are registered trademarks of Simon & Schuster, Inc.

ALADDIN M!X and related logo are registered trademarks of Simon & Schuster, Inc.

For information about special discounts for bulk purchases, please contact

Simon & Schuster Special Sales at 1-866-506-1949 or business@simonandschuster.com.

The Simon & Schuster Speakers Bureau can bring authors to your live event.

For more information or to book an event contact the Simon & Schuster Speakers

Bureau at 1-866-248-3049 or visit our website at www.simonspeakers.com.

Cover designed by Jessica Handelman

Interior designed by Mike Rosamilia

The text of this book was set in MrsEaves.

Manufactured in the United States of America 0917 OFF

10 9 8 7 6 5 4 3 2 1

This book has been cataloged with the Library of Congress.

ISBN 978-1-4814-8032-1 (hc)

ISBN 978-1-4814-8031-4 (pbk)

ISBN 978-1-4814-8033-8 (eBook)

For Josh . . . a supportive husband, an incredible father, and the most attentive proofreader I know.

chapter

* 1 *

IT'S A NORMAL WEDNESDAY MORNING, AND I DO WHAT I always do on normal Wednesday mornings. I sit at the kitchen table eating my Rice Krispies. Not on the couch while watching TV, like Coco does. Not standing at the counter while texting, like Eliza does. But at the table. Where one is supposed to eat one's breakfast.

As I bring the spoon up to my mouth, I listen for the snap-crackle-pop of my cereal. I've been eating Rice Krispies for breakfast every day since I had teeth, and the familiar sounds prepare me for my daily routine.

Dad is muttering something to the coffeepot while Mom is stuffing papers into her briefcase. It's an average, everyday, run-of-the-mill Wednesday.

"Darn it," Eliza screams, jumping back from the

kitchen counter, where she pushes her cereal bowl away from her.

"No need to yell, Eliza," Mom says, barely looking up from her briefcase.

"Well, what do you expect? I spilled milk all over my shirt." Eliza unrolls half of the paper towels on the roll hanging from the wall and wipes furiously at her stomach. "Oh, forget it." She throws the paper towels down. "I'm going to have to change."

"You'd better hurry up," Dad says. "We have to leave in five minutes."

"Five minutes?" Coco squeals. "My show won't be over by then."

"Sorry, kiddo," Dad says. "School trumps television."

"But I'll miss the best part." Coco slams her small fist down in her lap.

"You'll survive," Dad says.

"I can't believe this," Eliza says as she storms up the steps. "How am I going to get ready all over again in five minutes?"

Dad gives Mom "the look." They've been working on it since Eliza was my age. I think they've perfected it in the last four years.

"You'll have to deal with her," Mom hisses to Dad. "I'm late."

MOLLY IN THE MIDDLE

I finish my cereal, rinse my bowl, and put it neatly in the dishwasher.

"Let's go, kids," Dad calls as he pours his coffee into a to-go mug.

"Five more minutes?" Coco pleads.

"Now." Dad grabs his keys off the kitchen table, then stands at the bottom of the steps. "Eliza, we're leaving!"

"I'm not ready!" Eliza calls from upstairs. I hear the eye roll in her voice.

Dad looks at Mom again, but she just shrugs.

I take my backpack off the hook and sling it onto my shoulder. I'm the first one ready, as usual. Coco clicks the television off, but she leaves her cereal bowl in the middle of the floor. No wonder we're running low on bowls. I'll bet she has a collection under the couch. For such a little kid, she sure makes a huge mess.

Finally, Eliza comes down the steps. I do a double take when I see her. I shake my head. This isn't going to be good.

"Eliza," Dad snaps. "What do you think you're wearing?"

"What?" Eliza looks down at herself.

"You're wearing a . . . a . . . a nightie." Dad turns to yell for Mom. "Karen! Karen! Look what your daughter is wearing."

Mom joins us at the bottom of the steps.

* 3 *

"Eliza, you can't wear that to school." Mom uses her lawyer voice. The one you can't argue with.

"Why not?" Apparently, Eliza didn't get the memo about not arguing with Mom's lawyer voice.

"First of all"—Mom's tone remains calm—"it's against the dress code and they'll make you change."

"And second of all?" Eliza's hands are on her hips.

"Second of all," Mom begins, "if you walk out of the house like that, I'll ground you until you're thirty-two."

Eliza turns on her (very high) heels and stomps back up the steps, muttering about the absolute unfairness of life.

"That's how you have to deal with her," Mom tells Dad. She gives Coco and me a quick hug, grabs her briefcase, and bolts out the door.

She doesn't hug Dad.

Dad looks at his watch and sighs. It's nice that they drive us to school in the mornings since the bus comes so early, but sometimes I think getting up before the sun and taking the bus would just be easier. I take the bus in the afternoon because my parents are working, and it's not bad. It's more peaceful than being home sometimes.

I know Eliza will take forever to change, so I figure I'll clean up the mess that Coco left in the living room. I hang my backpack up, then head to the couch to deal

with Coco's latest disaster. I grab her bowl (which is on
its side, with white milk dribbling out onto the burgundy
area rug), spoon, juice cup, and crumpled-up napkin (at
least she used a napkin) and bring it all into the kitchen.

"I'll meet you in the car," Dad yells to all of us.

I run the water in the kitchen sink until it's hot. I
soap up the sponge and take care of Coco's sticky mess.
It feels good to put my hands under the running water—
it's calming somehow. I close my eyes and let the water
wash away the insanity that is my family's routine in the
morning.

Every morning.

Of every day of my life.

For the past twelve years.

When I feel Zen enough, I shut the water off and
dry my hands. I take my backpack off the hook and look
around the corner into the hallway. Nobody's there.

"Eliza?" I yell up the stairs.

Nothing.

They must have already gone to the car. I guess I didn't
hear them with the water running. A slight panic tugs at
my stomach—I don't want to be the reason we're late. I run
down the steps to the garage, and when I get there, I see
it's empty. Maybe the car's outside.

I bolt back up the steps and push open the front door.

As soon as I open it, I see Dad's car. It's pulling out of our driveway, onto the street.

My mouth opens, but no words come out. I just stand there, with my jaw practically touching the floor.

They left without me.

chapter

* 2 *

MY FEET ARE GLUED TO THE FLOOR. MY BRAIN ISN'T
quite comprehending what just happened.

Did they leave me here on purpose? Did I not get to
the car quickly enough? I can't believe Dad would do that.
I'm always the first one ready. We wait for Eliza every other
day. He wouldn't just leave me here as a punishment,
especially since I've never been late before.

The only other explanation is that they forgot me.

But of course they wouldn't *forget* me.

When my mind finally starts working again, I realize
I'm going to be late. And my class is taking a field trip to
the planetarium today. I've been looking forward to it all
week. I need a way to school, and I need it now.

I slide my cell phone out of my backpack pocket and

dial Dad's number. It goes straight to voice mail. Dad never keeps his phone on. He still insists on using our house phone—the one with a cord—whenever he makes a call. I can't call Eliza. Mom took her phone away for a week when she broke curfew. I dial Mom's number next.

"What's up, Molly?" The road hums in the background.

"Um." I still haven't completely processed what just happened. "Dad left without me."

There's a pause. And then Mom says, "What do you mean he left without you?"

"He said to meet him in the car, and when I got to the garage, they had already left." I pace in the front entryway.

"Oh, for crying out loud. And I assume his cell is off?"

"The phone went right to voice mail." I immediately regret calling her. Now she's going to be even more upset with Dad than she usually is.

"Great. Just great." I can practically hear Mom's blood pressure rise through the phone. "I don't have time to come back for you. I have to be in court this morning. Can you get another ride?"

I stare down at my shoes. I open my mouth to say something about the field trip, but I close it again before any words come out. She's already stressed, and I don't want to cause her to blow a gasket. "Yeah, Mom. I'm sure I can. I'll call a few friends."

"Good." Mom's tone radiates relief. "Call me if you have any problems."

I'm not sure what calling her will do. It's not like she would miss work to help me, but I agree anyway.

I hang up with her and call Kellan. He answers on the first ring.

"Hey, Mols. Shouldn't you be on your way to school?"

I take a deep breath. "My dad left without me."

"What?" Kellan's voice goes up an octave. "On purpose?"

"I don't know." My voice is quieter than I expect.

"Hang on. I'll see if my mom can come get you." I hear Kellan talking to his mom, and then he gets back on. "We'll be there in five."

My shoulders relax. "Thanks, Kels."

The house phone rings just as I put my cell phone back in my backpack. I run down the hall to pick it up.

"Hello?"

"Molly!" Dad's voice sounds frantic. "I'm so sorry. I'm on my way back to get you."

"Don't worry about it," I say. "I called Kellan, and Mrs. Bingham is going to come get me."

"Oh, that's good," Dad says. "I don't know what happened. We—we thought you were in the car. It wasn't until after I dropped Eliza off and headed to the middle school that we realized you weren't here."

"Oh," I say. Because I'm not sure what else to say. They actually *did* forget me.

"Really sorry, Molly."

"It's okay," I say. Even though it isn't okay at all.

"Thanks for being such a good sport," Dad says.

That's me. A good sport.

I hang up with Dad, grab my backpack, and wait on the front steps for Mrs. Bingham. They live only a few blocks away, so it isn't long until their SUV pulls into the driveway.

Kellan's in the front seat, but he gets out as I walk toward the car. He's moving slowly today, and his face flinches with every step he takes. He isn't wearing his leg braces.

"Kels," I yell to him. "Stay there. I can sit in the back."

"No worries." Kellan flashes me a smile. "You've had a rough morning."

But you've had a rough life, I think. I don't say it out loud. He hates when people feel sorry for him.

Instead of sitting in the front, I slide into the backseat next to him, my backpack on my lap. He smiles again, a crooked, grateful grin. We sat in the backseat together for years and years, until this year, when we were old enough to move up front. But it's not the same when one of us is in the front and one in the back.

"Thanks so much," I say to both Mrs. Bingham and Kellan. "You guys are lifesavers."

"Anytime, Molly," Mrs. Bingham says as she backs out of the driveway.

"My dad called." I look at Kellan. "He actually forgot me."

Kellan shakes his head. "He must have had a rough morning too."

"Just the usual. Eliza being Eliza. Coco being Coco."

Kellan nods. This is the beautiful thing about having the same best friend since preschool. I don't need to explain my crazy family to him.

"So what are you doing today?" I pull a piece of lint off my pants.

"I've got physical therapy in an hour," Kellan says. "And then Mom and I are going for a practice walk."

I snap my head up to look at him. "Without me?"

"Don't worry, Mols." Kellan puts his hand on my shoulder. "It's not like we won't practice again later. I need all the help I can get."

"I can't believe the walk is only a month away."

"I know. I think I'll be ready."

"You will be." I nod.

"As long as you're there to carry me if I can't make it."

I hit Kellan on the shoulder. "Yeah, right."

"I'm serious." Kellan's clear blue eyes shine, which lets me know he's not at all serious. "I expect you to carry me. On your back. For five miles."

"Forget it." I laugh. "I'll carry you mentally. How's that?"

"That's good," Kellan says, but his eyebrows are pinched together, so I know something's on his mind.

"But?" I ask.

He looks up at me. "But there's a possibility I may not be able to walk the whole way."

"That's okay." I give him my most reassuring smile. I've learned not to disagree with him when he says stuff like this, because he's right. There is a possibility he won't be able to walk the whole thing.

Kellan looks down at his hands. "I may need your help—you know—to push the wheelchair."

"Of course I'll help," I say. Kellan hates thinking about using a wheelchair, so I know it took a lot of courage for him to even bring it up. "But only if you promise to let me do some wheelies."

Kellan smiles and holds out his hand for me to shake. "Deal!"

We pull into Cherry Creek Middle School at exactly 8:12. I am officially twenty-two minutes late.

"Have a good day, Mols." Kellan gives me a fist bump. His eyes dart over to the school's entrance, and for a second his smile droops.

"You okay?" I ask, hand on the door handle.

"What?" He looks back over to me. "Oh, yeah, fine. Just thinking how happy I am that I don't have to be a part of the masses anymore."

"You're totally lucky," I say, and right now I mean it.

"Yeah." Kellan smiles back. "Totally."

I get out of the car and wave as Mrs. Bingham pulls away. Kellan is still staring out the window, watching me walk into school. He looks like a puppy dog that desperately wants to come out to play. I keep telling him he wouldn't like it anyway. It's not like it was in fifth grade, which was his last year in school. Middle school is way different. And not in a good way. There's more drama, more homework, and more kids. Things were simpler in fifth grade. Better.

Kellan didn't even need leg braces then.

I stop by the office for a late pass. Mrs. Clayton, the school secretary, looks up at me and squints her eyes.

"What's your name, hon?"

"Molly Mahoney."

She looks at me as if she's never seen me before.

"Mrs. Littman's seventh grade," I remind her.

"Oh no, hon." Her polite smile fades fast. "The

seventh grade just left for their field trip." She grabs the attendance sheet from a binder and points at it. "They said everybody was present."

I just stand there with my mouth hanging open.

"I'm really sorry, hon," Mrs. Clayton says. "Maybe you can sit in on one of the sixth-grade classes today."

I can't answer her because I can't think.

I can't talk.

I can't move.

I can't believe my class left without me.

Mrs. Clayton writes me a pass and tells me to go to Mr. Soto's room. Mr. Soto was my sixth-grade teacher last year. I have to spend the entire day with sixth graders learning things I already learned.

This is horrifying.

I stop in the bathroom on my way to Mr. Soto's and stand in front of the mirror. Maybe I turned invisible overnight.

I move my face closer to the mirror until my nose practically touches it.

There I am. Faded blue jeans, brown cardigan, white running shoes. My mousy brown hair hangs down like it usually does. I'm definitely not invisible. I look like everybody else.

And then it hits me.

MOLLY IN THE MIDDLE

I look like everybody else.

No wonder nobody sees me. Nothing stands out about me at all. I'm average. Ordinary. Humdrum.

I stare at myself in the mirror, and suddenly, I know what to do.

chapter

3

I RIDE MY BIKE OVER TO KELLAN'S AFTER SCHOOL. HE opens the front door just as I'm gliding down the driveway, and as soon as I spot the look on his face, my smile is gone.

Ugh. A total facepalm moment. How could I be so stupid?

"New bike?" He looks like Dad looks when he's on a diet and the rest of us are eating cookie-dough ice cream.

"No." I lean the bike against his garage. "It's Eliza's, but she said I could use it. She's too cool for bikes now, I guess."

"When did Eliza ever ride a Trek FX? That's like a five-hundred-dollar bike." Kellan makes his way around the bicycle, bending down to push on the pedals.

The pedals spin around and around. "She got it for her sixteenth birthday a few months ago. Mom and Dad thought it was because she was turning over a new leaf, getting into fitness and stuff, but really, Dave Delaney loved cycling, and she wanted to impress him." Dave Delaney lasted a week, and so did Eliza's bike.

Kellan's focus moves to the front wheel. He grimaces as he bends down, and every muscle in my body screams to stand behind him so that he doesn't fall. But I ignore my instincts and force myself to stay where I am. He wouldn't want me to baby him.

"I've always wanted a bike with an aluminum frame." Kellan holds on to the seat as he pushes himself up to standing. "How does she handle?"

"Fine." My weight shifts from one foot to the other. I scour my brain for other topics so we can change the subject. "Are you hungry?"

Kellan shrugs. "Not really."

"But I brought chocolate chip cookies." I dig into my backpack and pull out a Tupperware container.

"Mmm-hmm." But Kellan's not paying attention to the cookies. He's rambling on about mechanical disc brakes or botanical fish cakes or something like that.

"They're your favorite." I shove the Tupperware in front of his face and lift the lid so he can smell the chocolaty goodness. This seems to do the trick. He grabs the container, and I follow him into the house.

Mrs. Bingham is in the kitchen cutting fruit. She smiles when she sees me.

"Hiya, Molly." She holds out a bowl of sliced peaches. "Want some?"

"Molly brought cookies." Kellan holds up the Tupperware container. "Before you lecture me about too much sugar, we need to carbo load for our practice walk."

"At least have some green tea with those cookies." Mrs. Bingham puts a kettle of water on the stove. "Want some, Molly?"

"Sure," I say.

"You don't have to, Mols," Kellan whispers. "Mom's on a health kick."

"I actually like green tea," I whisper back. Kellan makes a face like he just sucked on a lemon dipped in hot sauce.

"Some studies have shown that green tea helps people with muscular dystrophy," Kellan tells me. "So guess who has to drink green tea until it comes out of his ears?"

I giggle, picturing green tea leaking out of Kellan's ears.

"She's also making me eat lots of plants." Kellan pops a cookie into his mouth, and as he chews, his eyes light up. "Chocolate is from the cocoa bean, right? That makes it a plant. Chocolate is healthy!"

"In that case, I'll have one." I grab a cookie out of the container and take a bite. We sip our green tea and chew our cookies in completely nonawkward silence. That's how it is when you've been best friends forever.

"All righty." Kellan wipes his face with a napkin. "Ready to roll?"

"Yep." I take our tea mugs over to the sink. Mrs. Bingham frowns when she sees Kellan's mostly untouched mug.

"Mom"—Kellan lifts himself out of his chair—"we're going out for a practice walk."

"Okay, have fun. I'll warm up your tea when you get back."

Walking with Kellan isn't like regular walking. We have to go slowly, and sometimes we even stop to rest. I don't mind, though, because we always have a lot to talk about. And today we have something pretty important to discuss.

"Your class left without you?" Kellan says, after I tell him how I had to spend the day in the sixth-grade classroom.

"Can you believe it?"

"What about Nina Chang? Didn't she tell the teacher you weren't there?"

I look down at my feet. "Nina and I aren't close anymore."

"What happened? I thought you two were pretty tight."

"We were. And then—I don't know. We weren't. She started hanging out with Christina."

"Ugh," Kellan yells. "Not Christina!"

"Yeah." I nod. "I don't get it either. I told you, middle school is weird."

"You weren't kidding." Kellan shakes his head. "Doesn't Nina remember that time Christina poured a whole container of salt into her water bottle during PE?"

I shrug.

"Or that time she taped toilet paper to the back of Nina's boots so Nina had a trail of TP following her all day?"

I wince at that memory. Nina cried in the bathroom for at least half an hour.

"Makes no sense," Kellan says, more to himself than to me.

"I wish you were still there." And the minute the words spill out of my mouth, I want to scoop them up, put them back in, and swallow them down.

Kellan nods. "Yeah, maybe soon."

"Really?" I practically jump out of my sneakers.

"My mom says physical therapy's been going really well. And I haven't been as tired lately. So, yeah, maybe."

"That would be awesome." I kick a pebble off of the sidewalk. "You know, when you're ready."

We walk in silence for a little while, until Kellan points to our usual break spot: a bench underneath a willow tree on the edge of our neighborhood park. I look at my watch. We've been walking for nine minutes.

It's warm for the middle of April, but it's cool and breezy under the tree. The air smells like spring—a combination of wet soil and blooming lilacs.

"So I'm thinking about changing some things about myself," I tell Kellan as we sit down.

"You're not going to get a tattoo, are you?" Kellan smiles, and I give him a nudge with my elbow.

"I hadn't thought about that, but it might help solve my problem."

"What problem?" Kellan squints at me.

"The problem of being totally and completely invisible." I stare down at the grass around my feet. It's a brighter green than it was last week.

"Is this because your parents forgot you this morning?"

"And because my class forgot me this morning."

Kellan nods. "I get it."

"So maybe I need to do something different. You know, to stand out more."

Kellan looks at me for a few seconds. "You could dye your hair purple."

I tilt my head and try to picture what that would look like. It would probably get me noticed.

"What is it that makes someone stand out, anyway?"

"I know!" Kellan points a finger in the air. "You can borrow my leg braces."

I actually gasp, but then I exhale when Kellan starts laughing. "Relax, Mols. I'm just kidding. But these things do get you noticed."

It's then that I realize Kellan and I have the exact opposite problem.

"Does it bother you?" I ask. "When people stare?"

He shrugs. "Not really. They're just curious. I'd be curious too."

I bend down and pick a dandelion out of the grass. "You probably think I'm a loser for wanting more attention."

"No way, Mols." Kellan shakes his head so hard that his hair falls into his eyes. "I would never think you're a loser."

I look up, expecting to find him laughing, but his face is totally serious. My cheeks burn, and I nudge him with my elbow again.

"I do think I could use a little makeover."

"Purple hair would be kind of cool." Kellan stares at the top of my head. "Or maybe rainbow. Rainbow hair."

"I'm being serious," I tell him.

He smiles. "So am I!"

"Really?"

"Sure," Kellan says. "Why not? If I saw somebody with rainbow hair, I'd definitely remember them. I'd notice if they were absent on field trip day."

I nod. Kellan may be onto something. A different hair color. It's not too crazy, but it's just crazy enough.

We continue on our walk, talking about the very noticeable hair color I could have (glow-in-the-dark green makes the top five), and by the time we get back to Kellan's house, we've walked for forty-three minutes, including three breaks of five minutes each. Beads of sweat cover the back of Kellan's neck, and I can tell by the way he's leaning against his front porch that he's tired. He'll never admit it, though.

"I should go." I point down the street, in the direction of my house. "My parents are probably home by now."

"Good luck with the new 'do," Kellan says as I get on my bike. "Come over tomorrow after school and show me the new you."

I stop by CVS on my way home and scan the hundreds of products in the hair-care aisle. There are rows and rows of normal-looking hair colors, but I finally find what I'm looking for on the bottom shelf. I pick up a multicolor streaking kit and read the back of the box. It says it contains everything I need to have rainbow hair. The price tag says $10.99. I keep $20 in my backpack in case of emergencies. This is definitely an emergency.

I purchase the kit, shove it into my backpack, and head for my house.

Everybody's home by the time I get there. Dad's in the kitchen cooking dinner. Mom's on her laptop at the dining room table. Coco is in front of the television. I don't see Eliza, but there's music blasting from her bedroom.

I hang my backpack up on the hook. I notice it's the only one there. Coco left hers on the floor, and Eliza stopped leaving her backpack downstairs months ago because she feels it's an invasion of privacy.

I walk into the kitchen, expecting Mom and Dad to run over to me, apologizing for what happened this morning. They'll probably give me a huge hug and maybe even a chocolate bar. They know how much I love chocolate bars.

"Hi, Molly," Dad says. "Would you mind grabbing the tomato sauce out of the fridge?"

I open the refrigerator, pull the jar out, and hand it to Dad.

"Thanks." He's humming while he throws pasta into a pot of boiling water.

"Hello, Molly." Mom walks into the kitchen and gives me a kiss on the top of my head. "Do you have homework?"

"A little."

"Why don't you start it now, before dinner?" She pours herself a glass of wine and goes back to the dining room table and her laptop.

I can't believe it. Nobody says anything. No apology, no hug, no chocolate bar.

I grab my homework out of my backpack and pull the CVS bag out with it. I can't help but wonder if rainbow hair will be enough.

I stare at my homework—a math sheet full of word problems. I've never missed a homework assignment before. But where has that gotten me? Forgotten and forced to spend the day with sixth graders, that's where. I shove the sheet back into my backpack and go up to my room, taking my rainbow-streaking hair kit with me.

chapter

* 4 *

SINCE ELIZA HOGGED THE BATHROOM AFTER DINNER
last night with her two-hour bubble bath, I get up extra early
to do my hair this morning before school. I need to be sure
I'm out of the bathroom before anyone is awake. The sun is
barely up as I take the hair-streaking kit into the bathroom
and lock the door. I open up the directions, put on the plastic gloves that are included, and get to work. As instructed,
I divide my hair into sections and use a different bottle on
each one. Then I repeat the process until my entire head is
covered. I sit there and let the color soak in for thirty minutes. Good thing Eliza leaves magazines in the bathroom.
I leaf through them until the "color development" time is
up. The last step is to wash the color out, so I jump in the
shower and watch rainbow streaks swirl down the drain.

After I towel off my hair and blow it dry, I spend five minutes staring in the mirror. I hardly recognize myself. My hair is streaked with purple, green, yellow, blue, and red. My stomach does a little flip when I wonder what everyone will say when they see it.

The house is still quiet when I leave the bathroom, so I tiptoe to my bedroom. I open my closet to get dressed, but none of my old clothes match my new hair. I open all of my drawers and rifle through every piece of clothing I own. Nothing seems to work. Compared to my hair, my clothes are dull and boring.

The shower turns on in the bathroom next door, and I know Eliza will be in there for a while. I open my door and sprint down the hall toward her bedroom. I turn the doorknob slowly, look around to make sure nobody sees me, then push the door open just enough to squeeze through.

Her room screams chaos.

It's not that it's messy, like Coco's. Eliza's actually pretty organized. It's just that there's so much going on in one small space. Every inch of her walls is covered. There are posters of bands she likes, pictures of her friends, and even a big sign that says IF YOU CAN READ THIS, GET OUT OF MY ROOM! That one makes the hair on the back of my neck stand up. She would probably kill me if she found me in here.

I open her closet, which is packed with clothes. Some are hanging neatly on hangers, others are folded and kept in bins on the floor. I can't wear something she wears often since she would definitely miss it, so I open the bins on the floor and look for something I haven't seen recently.

It turns out I have a lot to choose from. Eliza keeps every piece of clothing she's ever owned. I even find stuff in my size buried in one of the bottom bins. I settle on a hot pink T-shirt and lime green leggings. I put all the bins back where they belong and close the closet door.

I'm about to leave her room when I spot another bin on top of her desk. This one is smaller and clear, and it's filled with makeup.

I've never worn makeup before, but as I peer into the bin at all those tubes of lipstick, I decide that a little makeup might complete the look. And there's no way she would notice if anything was missing. She's got enough makeup in here for seventeen faces.

I choose a light pink lip gloss and a tube of black mascara. Standing in front of Eliza's makeup mirror, I brush my lips with the gloss and then squeeze them together like I've seen some girls do when they put on lipstick. My lips feel so sticky and weird that I'm tempted to wipe it off, but I don't. I open the mascara, put my face as close to the mirror as I can, and swipe the inky gunk onto my eyelashes. This takes longer than expected, since I blink every time the mascara wand gets close to my eyes.

I'm closing the tube when I realize that the shower is no longer on.

Eliza will be out any minute.

My first instinct is to hide in her closet, but there's no room in there with all those bins. I contemplate sliding under the bed, but if I do that, I'll never be ready in time. Eliza will stay in her room until it's time to leave for school. I have to get out of here, and I have to do it now.

I grab the clothes and makeup and open her bedroom door just enough to see the bathroom door. It's still closed. I hold my breath, close her bedroom door, and sprint back into my room as fast as I can.

Once I'm safe in my bedroom, I exhale. I move my desk chair and wedge the top of it underneath the doorknob so no one can come in. Our doors don't have locks, and Coco has a habit of walking in without knocking.

After I'm dressed in my new clothes, I look in the full-length mirror inside my closet door.

"Wow," I say out loud.

I look different.

I look cool.

I look like someone who isn't going to be forgotten.

I'm about to head downstairs for breakfast when it hits

me that I have no idea how my parents are going to react when they see me. Will they ground me? Make me change my clothes like they do to Eliza? Keep me home from school until the rainbow dye washes out? I take a deep breath and exhale all of my nervousness. If they do any of those things, at least they're noticing me. And that's what I'm going for after all.

I take one last look in the mirror before turning on my heels, holding my head up high, and marching downstairs to face my family.

When I reach the kitchen, I head straight to the cupboard to pull out my Rice Krispies, just like I do every other day. Everyone is where they always are at breakfast—Coco's in front of the TV, Mom is getting ready for work, and Eliza's still upstairs. The only person at the table is Dad, who is sipping coffee and reading the newspaper.

I take my regular seat and begin to eat, glancing up from my bowl every few seconds to see if anybody has noticed my new look.

After I'm halfway through my breakfast, I look up to find Dad staring at me. I swallow a spoonful of cereal and give him a weak smile.

"What happened to your hair?" He takes a sip of coffee.

"Oh. This?" My hand flies up to the top of my head. "I just thought I'd try something different."

Dad stares at me for a little while longer. "It's cute."

It's *cute*?

Mom walks in just as I'm thinking of something to say. I had all sorts of awesome comebacks for what I thought he'd say, such as:

It's my hair. I can do what I want to it.

Eliza colored her hair when she was my age.

What's the big deal? It's just hair!

But I have no responses for, *It's cute.*

"What the—" Mom stops in her tracks when she sees me. "What did you do to your hair?"

Now, this is more like it.

"What's the big deal? It's just hair." I sit up taller in my seat.

"Are you wearing makeup?" Mom walks toward me, squinting.

"A little."

Here it comes.

"Awww." Mom pats me on the head. "I think it's nice that you're finally dressing up, Molly. It's a cute look for you."

"That's what I said," Dad chimes in.

Seriously? This is the one thing in the entire world that they actually agree on?

"You mean I'm not in trouble?"

Mom chuckles. "Why would you be in trouble?"

"I didn't ask first," I say.

Mom shrugs. "That stuff washes out pretty quickly. It's no big deal."

It's no big deal.

My stomach drops to my knees, and I can feel the Rice Krispies snap-crackle-popping all the way to my toes.

Eliza stomps down the stairs in her too-short skirt, looks me up and down, and rolls her eyes. She then proceeds to the kitchen counter, where she pours Cocoa Puffs into a Ziploc bag. She doesn't say anything—not about my hair and not about the clothes that she hopefully doesn't recognize anymore; in fact, she doesn't even look at me again.

"Okay, kids." Dad gets up from the table and puts his coffee mug in the sink. "Time to go."

Wait. What? I was so busy worrying about what my parents would say that I completely forgot that I actually have to go to school looking like this.

Will my classmates think my look is *no big deal*? Will they think it's *cute*?

Will they even notice?

chapter

* 5 *

JUST AS I DO EVERY DAY, I WALK PAST KIDS IN THE
hallway as I make my way toward my locker. Something's
different today, though.

Some kids whisper and point. Some kids stare. People
are actually looking at me, which has never, ever happened
before ever in my life.

I turn the combination on my locker and pull out
my language arts notebook. Just as I'm about to close my
locker, two figures appear on either side of me. I know
who it is even before I look up. The overwhelming smell
of perfume fills my lungs, and I have to stifle a cough.

"Well," Christina says, leaning against the locker next
to mine, "what's with the new look?"

I turn around to find Nina on the other side of me,

staring . . . and smiling. "I like it. Your hair is really cool."

"Oh." I touch the tip of a green strand. "Thanks."

"And I love how it totally matches your outfit." Nina's eyes blink, making her silver sparkly eye shadow shimmer under the fluorescent light of the hallway.

"So what's the deal?" Christina's still leaning against the locker next to mine, arms crossed in front of her.

I shrug. "No deal."

Christina looks at me like she's waiting for me to say something else, but I really don't know what to say.

"Hmmm." Christina tilts her head like she's trying to solve for *X* in algebra. "Come on, Nina, we've got to get to class."

"Later," Nina says as she follows Christina down the hallway.

"Bye," I say, although by the time the word comes out, they're out of earshot.

When I arrive at language arts class, it's pretty apparent that Christina and Nina aren't the only ones who notice my hair.

"Ms. Mahoney, is that you?" Mrs. Littman squints her eyes in my general direction.

"Ummm." I look around to be sure I'm the only Ms. Mahoney in the room. "Yes, it's me."

She purses her lips and shakes her head as she checks

off the attendance sheet. At least she doesn't say anything else about my new look. I take my seat as the chatter buzzes around me.

"Settle down, settle down." Mrs. Littman takes her glasses off and places them gently on the corner of her desk. "Now please turn to page thirty-two of your workbook. Today we'll be working on—"

The classroom door flies open, and Robert Jackson bolts in.

"Sorry I'm late, Mrs. Littman." Robert closes the door behind him. "You'll never guess what happened to me on the way to school today."

"Your late pass, Mr. Jackson?" Mrs. Littman holds out her hand.

Robert dumps everything he's carrying—his backpack, lunch, jacket, and, for some reason that only he understands, an enormous plastic tarantula—onto the ground. He fishes around in the pocket of his jeans until he pulls out a crumpled blue slip, which he hands to Mrs. Littman.

"That's the second time this month." Mrs. Littman lets out a little tsk-tsk sound as she reopens her attendance book.

"At least I'm consistent." As usual, he's smiling. Robert Jackson is always smiling. He has super-white teeth.

"Yes, you are." Mrs. Littman sighs. "Please take your seat."

Robert grabs his belongings off the floor and heads to his seat, which happens to be right behind mine. He puts his jacket on the back of his chair, places the plastic tarantula on the corner of his desk, and rummages through his backpack for at least a minute before he finds his workbook, which is missing the cover page.

"Whoa," Robert says, tapping me on the shoulder with his pencil. I turn around.

"What'dya do to your hair?"

I'm pretty sure, based on the amount of heat I feel in my cheeks, that my face is on fire. Robert Jackson is notorious for thinking out loud. If it's in his head, it's out his mouth. I've always admired that about him—from afar. Although Robert has a lot to say, he's never actually said anything to me.

"Mr. Jackson," Mrs. Littman snarls, "it's bad enough that you're late, but you don't need to disrupt Ms. Mahoney. Now please turn to page thirty-two and pay attention to the lesson."

"But I just wanted to know what—"

"Page thirty-two, Mr. Jackson. Now."

I sink a little lower in my chair. Of course I wanted to be noticed. I mean, that's why I colored my hair and wore different clothes. But I didn't plan for people asking me about it. I certainly didn't plan for *Robert Jackson* to ask me about it. Robert is probably the most popular boy in school. He's funny and cute and the best soccer player in the entire seventh grade. In all the years we've been in class together, we haven't said one word to each other.

Until today.

Mrs. Littman is going on and on about sentence structure, but I can't focus on anything she says. Instead, I twirl a chunk of purple hair around my fingers and stare down at my workbook until all the words blur together into a black-and-white blob. Robert Jackson noticed me. Robert Jackson talked to me. Robert Jackson is poking me with his pencil again.

I turn around, and he mouths something I can't understand. I glance back at Mrs. Littman. Luckily, she's writing something on the whiteboard, her back turned to us.

"I can't hear you," I whisper to Robert.

Robert leans forward, his elbows resting on the edge of his desk. "I said, it would be great if—"

"Mr. Jackson and Ms. Mahoney!" Mrs. Littman's voice echoes off of the walls. I snap my head around and turn in my seat so I'm facing forward.

"If I have to remind you again, Mr. Jackson, you can do all the talking you'd like in the principal's office." And then she glares at me. "It seems that hair color has done something to your brain, Ms. Mahoney."

A cold sweat breaks out on my neck. I've never gotten yelled at by a teacher before. I have no idea what I'm supposed to do, so I just stare at my hands, which are folded neatly on my desk.

Someone snickers to my left. Christina. I steal a glance behind me to see a smug look on her face, and I'm sure she's feeling reassured that the only thing different about me is my hair. I'm still a nobody who doesn't deserve to be in her atmosphere.

Anger bubbles in my stomach, and before I realize what I'm doing, words pour out of my mouth.

"You'd look good with rainbow hair, Mrs. Littman."

The entire class is still. I'm not sure if anyone is even breathing.

"What did you say?" Mrs. Littman looks confused, like she must have heard me wrong. I know I shouldn't say anything. Maybe it's not too late to take it back, to apologize, or to deny I even said it in the first place.

But then everyone in this class will go back to forgetting about me. They'll just think I'm some loser with weird hair.

I swallow the fear that's formed a ball in my throat. It hurts going down, but I have no other choice. I can't turn back now. "I said that you'd look good with rainbow hair."

The class erupts in laughter, but Mrs. Littman clearly doesn't see the humor.

"Ms. Mahoney." She's standing so close to me now that I can smell the laundry detergent on her clothes. "Since this is your first offense, I will let it slide. I won't be so kind next time."

I nod and hope that my quivering chin lets her know that I didn't really mean it. Mrs. Littman isn't a bad teacher, and besides the fact that she's totally boring, I've never had anything against her. Mrs. Littman raises her eyebrows, threatening me to say something else, but I don't. I just slide lower in my chair and wait for her to resume her lesson. I barely move for the rest of the class, too terrified that she'll make good on her promise about the "next time" I get in trouble.

I'm so tense that the sound of the bell actually makes me jump in my seat. There's another tap on my shoulder, which I pretend not to notice. What in the wild world would I say to Robert Jackson that could possibly be coherent and charming? And even though class is technically over, I'm still in Mrs. Littman's room.

Tap. Tap. Tap. "Hey," he says. "Molly, right?"

He knows my name?

I turn around slowly as I slide my workbook into my backpack.

"Your hair. It's totally rad." He leans back in his chair and taps his pencil on his desk, an adorable grin on his face.

"Thanks." I grab my backpack and practically sprint to the door. I won't be able to relax until I'm out of this classroom.

Robert catches up to me in the hallway, running his hands through his shaggy blond hair. "Maybe you could do mine?"

"Uhhh, okay." I try not to smile, but I can't help it. Robert Jackson is swoonworthy.

"Sweet!" He fist bumps the air. "And how about what you said to Mrs. Littman?"

My stomach drops. "I know. It just sort of came out and—"

"It was epic." He's beaming, looking at me like I just canceled school for the rest of the month.

Just as I'm about to answer, a couple of other boys from the class come by and pat me on the shoulder.

"Nice comeback," one of them says.

"Cool hair," adds the other.

Robert fist bumps them both.

"I gotta get to class," Robert says. "But let's stay in touch about the hair, okay?"

And then he's gone.

MOLLY IN THE MIDDLE

I'm left standing alone in the hallway, replaying the last hour in my mind.

Is it possible that rainbow hair and an off-the-cuff comment to a teacher could completely change my life? There's one thing I know for sure: this day is off to a memorable start.

chapter
* 6 *

I SPEND MY LUNCH PERIOD IN THE LIBRARY. EVER
since I started middle school and Kellan started home-
schooling, there hasn't been anyone to spend lunch with.
Sometimes we hung out with Nina, but that was before she
became BFFs with Christina.

We're not supposed to have our phones at school, but
I take a peek at mine as I pull my PB&J sandwich out of my
backpack. There's a text from Kellan.

How's the hair?

I look around to be sure the librarian isn't looking,
then I snap a selfie and send it to him. My phone vibrates
a few seconds later.

WOW! U look AMAZING. Come over after school so I can
see it 4 real.

I can't help but laugh out loud, even as I swallow the lump that has made itself at home in my throat. I miss Kellan. I miss having a best friend at school. I look around at the other kids eating lunch in the library. There are only a handful of us, and it's the same kids every day. Maybe we can get together and form a little club: Losers Without Lives. But most of them have their heads buried in books, like they're happy for some peace and quiet.

I roll my eyes at myself. *Snap out of it, Molly!* If Kellan doesn't feel sorry for himself, then I certainly shouldn't feel sorry for myself. He's the one with the real problems, and he never complains or feels bad about his situation. Sometimes I wish I could be more like Kellan.

I guess the novelty of my new 'do and my sassy remarks has worn off, because nobody else says anything to me about it for the rest of the day. I'm climbing the steps to my bus when someone yells my name. I whip my head around to find Robert running toward me. The kids behind me are pushing and shoving, so I have no choice but to move forward. The bus doors swoosh shut, and the driver tells us to find a seat. I slide into an empty seat and peer out the window. Robert points to his hair with a questioning grin on his face. I smile, and my head gives a slight nod. He gives me a thumbs-up before running off.

Does this really mean what I think it means? Robert

Jackson wants me to help him look . . . like me? This is something that would have seemed impossible just yesterday.

I run from my bus stop to my house, grab my bike, and pedal as fast as I can to Kellan's. I can't wait to tell him about my day.

"It looks even better in person," he says as he opens the door. "Turn around."

I spin in circles on his front porch. If I go fast enough, maybe the colors will whirl together like a rainbow tornado.

"Amazing." He looks like he's never seen me before. "It just brightens up your whole face."

"It's been a crazy day," I tell him. "Want to go for a training walk and I'll tell you about it?"

Kellan's smile disappears for a fraction of a second. If I didn't know him so well, I wouldn't have even noticed.

"Hang on," he says. "Let me just tell my mom."

I step into the entryway as he shuffles down the hallway, slower than usual, and makes his way around the corner. He's talking to his mom in a low voice, and I can't hear what they're saying. He comes back into the hallway, his mother following behind him.

"Hi, Molly," she says. "I just wanted to let you know—"

She stops talking when she looks up at me, her mouth still hanging open.

"Hi, Mrs. Bingham." I can't seem to look her in the eye, so I focus on my shoelaces.

"Doesn't her hair look great, Mom?" Kellan asks.

Mrs. Bingham tilts her head. "It's very colorful."

"Thank you," I say, because I'm not sure what else to say. I wonder if she meant that as a compliment.

"Come on, Mols," Kellan says. "Let's get that walk in."

"Just one minute," Mrs. Bingham says. "Molly, Kellan hasn't been feeling well today, so be sure he takes it easy, okay?"

"Mom." Kellan rolls his eyes. "I'm fine."

"Maybe you can take the wheelchair. It will be good practice for—"

"Mom." Kellan grits his teeth. "I'm *fine.*"

Mrs. Bingham nods her head once. "Just take it slow."

"We will." This time I look right into her eyes, so she knows she can count on me.

I can tell Kellan is struggling even before we get out of his driveway. Not only is he moving slowly, but his fists are clenched, which always means he's not feeling well.

I stop walking and gently grab his arm. "We don't have to do this today, you know."

"Why not? Aren't you up for it?" Kellan gives me a lopsided smile.

"Your mom said you're not feeling well."

"Yeah, well, my mom also said that chocolate chip cookies are toxic, so obviously, she can't be trusted." He chuckles. "And anyway, the walk is less than a month away. I've got a lot of training to do."

"Okay." I start walking again. "But we can go back for the wheelchair."

"I'm fine." He looks at me and raises his eyebrows. "Promise me you won't turn into my mom."

"Scout's honor." I hold up three fingers, hoping that's the right symbol. Brownies was a long time ago.

"If she thinks I'm feeling bad, she won't ever let me go back to school."

"Have you been talking more about it?"

"Are you kidding? I only bring it up every single day."

"Don't worry," I say. "Your charm will wear her down eventually."

"That's what I'm counting on," Kellan says.

"So I think the name of our team should be the Chocolate Chip Cookies," I say.

"That's perfect!" Kellan nods.

"Great! I'll design the shirt for us." I clap my hands with excitement.

"Cool! But first you have to fill me in on all the gossip of the day." Kellan elbows me in the side. "I can't wait to hear."

I spend the next fifteen minutes blabbing about everyone's reactions to my new look—my parents, Christina, Nina, Mrs. Littman, and, of course, Robert Jackson.

"Robert Jackson wants to have rainbow hair, huh?" Kellan nods his head. "I could totally see that."

"Yeah, but he wants *me* to help him," I say. "How crazy is that?"

"That's wild," Kellan says. "Are you going to?"

I shrug. "Who knows. He could forget all about it by tomorrow."

We reach the bench, and Kellan winces as he lowers himself onto it. I slide in next to him. I want to ask him how he's feeling, but I won't. It would just annoy him.

We sit in silence for a little while, until Kellan looks up at me, all serious-like.

"I have something really important to ask you," he says.

My stomach twists, and I nod. "Of course."

He looks at me for a couple seconds longer. "Do you have any cookies on you? My mom's killing me with this diet of hers."

He laughs and laughs, and I hit him lightly on the shoulder.

"You scared me for a minute." My heart rate slows down to normal speed.

"I know. I'm sorry. But I'm totally serious." His eyebrows furrow. "I really need a cookie."

"Come on." I stand up and offer him my hand. "Let's get you a cookie."

"You're a lifesaver, you know that. Team Chocolate Chip Cookies to the rescue." Kellan takes my hand, and I pull him up. He's tired. I can tell by his slumped shoulders and slow pace.

"Today was a long day," I say as I link my arm in his. "I might need some help. How about if you pull me along?"

"Sure thing, Lazypants," Kellan says. I let him lean on me, holding his arm up with my elbow. He knows I'm helping him, and I know I'm helping him, but we don't say a word about it.

chapter

* 7 *

I HEAR THE YELLING COMING FROM UPSTAIRS EVEN before I walk in the front door.

Mom and Dad are at it again. I tiptoe into the house and try to make my way to my room before anyone sees me, but Coco turns around just as I'm heading up the stairs. I'm surprised she was able to peel herself away from the TV long enough to even notice.

"Don't go into Mom and Dad's room. They're having a discussion." She puts air quotes around the word "discussion."

"Yeah, I can hear that."

Coco turns back toward the television, her hand reaching into a bag of greasy potato chips.

I try not to listen to the words coming from my

parents' bedroom, but even with their door closed, it's kind of hard to ignore that level of noise.

"Maybe if you didn't bury yourself in work all the time, you'd be able to help around here," Dad says.

"The reason I work all the time is so we can afford your nice car and your expensive golf vacations," Mom counters in her lawyer voice. I grimace. Once she brings out the lawyer voice, Dad is doomed.

"I haven't been on a golf vacation in months," Dad says.

"That's only because you hurt your back," Mom says. "Don't act like you're sacrificing for your family."

"What would you know about sacrificing for your family?" Dad's voice is high-pitched. "You haven't cared about this family in years. All you care about is making partner."

"Well, at least I'd be a partner in *something*."

I stick my fingers in my ears as I practically run to my room. Once I'm there, I close the door, grab my iPod, and put my headphones in. I find the most upbeat music on my playlist and turn the volume up as high as it will go. I'll probably break my eardrums, but on the bright side, I won't be able to hear my parents fight anymore.

I lie on my bed and close my eyes. I'm not sure how long I stay there, but after several songs someone opens my door.

"Hey," I say even before I turn around to see who it is, "why don't you knock?"

I take my headphones out and find Eliza standing in my doorway.

"I did knock, you loser. You didn't hear me."

"Oh." I sit up. "Sorry."

She looks terrible. Her black eyeliner is smeared, like maybe she's been crying. But I haven't seen Eliza cry since she was eight years old and Tommy Watson punched her in the nose for calling him a poopyhead.

"Dad wants to know what you want on your pizza." She crosses her arms in front of her.

"We're having pizza?"

Eliza shrugs. "It would seem that way."

"Onions, green peppers, and pineapple."

Eliza's lip curls. "That's disgusting."

And then she leaves my room, slamming the door behind her.

The light outside is fading, and the blue paint on my walls looks more like a sickly shade of gray. I love my room. It's the one place in my house where I feel like I really belong. My parents let me redecorate for my eleventh birthday, and I chose a tropical theme. Pictures of beaches and palm trees line the walls, and my bedspread and pillows are covered with schools of colorful tropical fish. It's usually so bright and happy, but tonight it just looks dull and murky, like the bottom of the deep, dark ocean.

I lie in bed with my eyes closed until I hear the doorbell ring and Coco yells "Pizza!" at the top of her lungs. I drag myself downstairs because, despite the dingy tone of the night, I do love pizza.

Dad places a pile of paper plates in the middle of the table. "Dig in."

Coco already has two slices of pepperoni in front of her. I find the onion, green pepper, and pineapple pie and slide a piece onto my plate. The cheese is extra thick and gooey, just the way I like it.

"Where's Eliza?" Dad asks as he pours himself a glass of ginger ale.

I take a bite of pizza and shrug.

"Can you please tell Eliza dinner is here?" Dad asks Coco.

Coco wipes her greasy hands on a paper towel and yells, "ELIZA! Dinner's here!"

"I could have done that," Dad says. "Please go upstairs and get her."

"Why do I have to go?" Coco whines. "Molly's older."

Dad sighs, then looks at me. "Molly, can you please go get Eliza?"

I'm not sure how me being older has anything to do with going upstairs, but I don't argue with either of them. There's been enough arguing in this house for one day.

I knock on Eliza's door.

She opens it and glares at me. "What?"

"Pizza is here," I say.

"Fine." And then she closes the door in my face.

I go back to the kitchen and sit down. "I told her."

"Is she coming?" Dad asks.

"I guess so," I say. Why does Dad care so much if Eliza eats with us? Most of the time she eats ramen noodles over the sink for dinner. Our family isn't the type to sit down together for long meals.

I'm on my second slice by the time Eliza gets to the table. "Where are the mozzarella sticks?"

"Check the bag. It's still on the counter," Dad says.

Eliza pulls a silver container out of the paper bag on the counter and brings it to the table. She pulls a mozzarella stick out and takes a bite but doesn't offer one to anyone else.

Dad pushes his plate away and clears his throat. "Girls, I need to talk to you about something."

I look at him, but Eliza and Coco keep eating.

"Your mom went to stay with Aunt Kathy for a few days."

"Why?" Coco asks, a mouth full of pizza.

"She just needed some time away," Dad says.

"Away from what?" Coco asks.

"You, probably," Eliza huffs.

Dad shoots her a look. "She just needs some privacy to get some work done."

"But how can she have privacy if Aunt Kathy's there?" Coco asks.

"OMG, Coco," Eliza says. "You are so dense."

"Eliza." Dad glares at her. "Enough."

"When's she coming back?" The pizza sits like a brick in my stomach.

"In a few days," Dad says. "Probably in a few days."

It's not that strange for Mom to be gone. She's hardly ever home in time for dinner, and she takes a lot of business trips. But it feels weird that she's not working or traveling and is staying at Aunt Kathy's. She and Dad must have had a major fight.

"Whatever," Eliza says. "I'm going to eat these in my room." She takes the container of mozzarella sticks and stomps up the steps.

"If Eliza doesn't have to eat at the table," Coco begins, "neither do I, right? I'm going to watch TV."

Dad shakes his head, but more to himself than to her. Coco takes another piece of pizza and brings her plate to the living room.

MOLLY IN THE MIDDLE

"Take your time, Molly," Dad says as he gets up from the table. "I have some work to catch up on."

"That's okay," I say. "I'm done anyway." I push my half-eaten slice of pizza away from me. I'm just not hungry anymore.

There's a text from Mom waiting for me when I get back up to my room.

Hi, Molly. I'm going to pick you up from school tomorrow. We can get ice cream.

Ice cream? My mom doesn't eat ice cream. And she never, ever picks me up from school.

This *can't* be good.

chapter

8

I HIT SNOOZE SEVEN TIMES BEFORE GETTING OUT OF bed the next day. I woke up so often in the middle of the night, I don't have the energy to sneak back into Eliza's room for more clothes today. I find a pair of ripped jeans in my closet that could look kinda cool (I ripped them when I fell off of my bike, but nobody has to know that) and a bright pink hoodie that Aunt Kathy got me for my birthday but I never wore before because it's so . . . bright. It turns out bright pink looks great with rainbow hair, so I throw it on.

Nobody says anything on the car ride to school. I did notice that Eliza's skirt is shorter than usual, but Dad didn't comment. I guess he feels like he can't get anywhere without Mom backing him up, and he's probably right.

When I get to my locker, Robert is leaning against it.

"Hey," he says when he sees me. "I've been waiting for you."

Robert Jackson is waiting for me?

"Oh," I say, which is the most brilliant thing I can come up with on such short notice.

"Are you doing anything this weekend?" He raises his eyebrows.

"Hmmm," I say. I hope this makes it seem like I'm mentally going through my busy social calendar rather than buying time to think of something to say. "I'm not sure yet. Still firming up plans."

"That's cool." Robert leans against the locker next to mine. "I was hoping you might be able to help me with my hair."

It takes every ounce of energy I have to keep my feet on the floor. I want to jump up and down and scream *YESSSSSSSSSS!* as loud as I can. Instead, I nod, maybe a little too enthusiastically. "Sure, we can do that."

"Yeah?" Robert's face brightens.

"Yeah." I can't help but smile.

"Sweet!" He pulls a pen out of his back pocket and grabs my hand.

OMIGOSH, ROBERT JACKSON IS HOLDING MY HAND.

Well, not holding it really. More like holding on to it, so he can write something on my palm.

"This is my number. Text me when you know what time you're free."

"I will." My voice comes out like a squeak. I clear my throat.

"Cool. It's a date." And then he runs off.

It's a date? Did I just make a date with Robert Jackson?

My mind is whizzing so fast that I barely notice Christina and Nina running toward me. Nina grabs my hand.

"OMG! Did Robert Jackson just give you his number?"

"Uhhhh." I stare at the numbers on my hand. "I think so."

"Nice," Christina says. "Half the girls in this school would kill for those digits. I, of course, have them, but hardly anyone else does."

Nina gives me a wink. "He's really cool, Molly."

"Hey," Christina says, "why don't you sit with us today at lunch?"

First Robert gives me his number, and then Christina invites me to sit with her at lunch? I lean against my locker because I don't trust my own legs to hold me up right now.

"You totally should," Nina says.

"Great." I smile. "Thanks."

The bell rings, and Christina and Nina take off down

the hallway. I grab the books I need for first period and then pre-algebra and practically run to class. My feet don't touch the ground the entire way.

At lunchtime I walk toward the cafeteria (and past the library) with a bounce in my step. I open the door, and the noise nearly pushes me over. It's been so long since I've been in a school cafeteria, I forgot how loud it can be. I also forgot how smelly it can be. Today's scent is eau de refried beans. At least I hope that's what I'm smelling.

Nina sees me lingering in the doorway and waves me over. I hold tightly to my boring brown paper bag and force myself to put one foot in front of the other. My stomach feels like it's trying to exit my body and take off without me, but I'm not sure if it's nerves or excitement.

"Hi, Molly." Nina pats the chair next to hers. "You can sit here."

"Thanks." I make my body as small as possible as I slide into the chair, careful not to take up too much space in a place I'm not yet sure I belong.

"Molly, you know Devon and Izzy, right?" Nina points to the other two girls sitting at the table.

Izzy tilts her head and squints at me. "What was your name again?"

"Molly." I've been going to school with Izzy since kindergarten.

"Right." Izzy smiles. "It's really nice to meet you. I totally love your hair."

"And I loved that you sassed Littman yesterday," Christina says.

"You sassed Littman?" Izzy leans forward, anxious to hear more.

"Not really." I can feel my face heating up. "I mean, it wasn't much."

"Yeah, it was," Christina says. "She told her she would look good with rainbow hair."

"No way!" Izzy throws her head back and laughs. "You said that?"

"She totally did," Christina says.

"That's awesome," Devon pipes in. "I wish I were there."

"So, what's going on with you and Robert?" Christina is peeling an orange.

"Not much," I say. Truth is, I have no idea what's going on between me and Robert.

"Is something going on with you and Robert?" Devon's eyes grow to three times their normal size.

"He gave her his number this morning," Christina tells her.

"No. Way. Are you going to text him?" Now Devon leans forward in her chair.

I look at the phone number written on my hand. "I guess so."

"You totally have to," Nina says. "He's so cute."

"So cute," Devon agrees.

They spend the next twenty minutes telling me how awesome Robert is, which I pretty much already know. But I really don't care what they talk about. It's so nice to eat lunch with somebody for a change, and by the time the bell rings, my insides feel all warm. I'm not sure if it's the hot chocolate I drank, or if maybe, just maybe, I finally belong somewhere at this school.

The gushy feeling doesn't last for long. At dismissal I remember that Mom is picking me up for our ice-cream date. I go out the front door, and instead of turning right toward the buses, I turn left toward the parking lot.

Robert is already there with a couple of other boys. They're skateboarding up and down the ramps.

I don't want him to think I'm following him, so I pretend to be fascinated with a speck of dirt on my shoe.

"Hey, Molly." He skates up to me.

"Oh, hi, Robert." I look up at him like he's the last person in the world I expected to see. Mom's car pulls up to the curb.

"Totally stoked about getting together this weekend." He's rocking back and forth on his skateboard. If I tried to do that, I'd fall flat on my face.

"Oh, yeah, me too." My heart is beating so fast that I start to feel dizzy.

"Wanna try?" Robert jumps off his skateboard and flips it up so that he's now holding it out to me.

"Oh, I would but—" I watch my Mom's car come to a stop. "My mom's here."

"Cool," Robert says. "Don't forget to text me."

"Sure."

He hops on his skateboard and rides away. I open the passenger door of Mom's car and slide in.

"Friend of yours?" Mom motions toward Robert with her eyes.

"Kind of," I answer. I close my hand into a fist so she doesn't see the writing on my palm.

"Mmm-hmm." Mom doesn't say anything else, but she's grinning. She probably thinks I like Robert, which obviously, I don't. I'm just helping him with his hair. I mean, I guess I *could* like him, but we just started talking a day ago. Sheesh. Why do grown-ups always jump to conclusions?

"What do you think about Clearville Creamery?" Mom pulls into their parking lot before I can even answer.

I order a double scoop of vanilla with rainbow sprinkles, and Mom orders coffee. Not even coffee ice cream, but actual coffee. And she drinks it without cream or sugar. Ew.

"Why don't you eat ice cream?" I ask when we find a booth in the corner.

"Sugar makes me feel sluggish. Coffee keeps me alert. And for my job I need to be alert."

I take small bites of my ice cream, making sure a few rainbow sprinkles make it into every spoonful. Mom just sips her coffee and watches me. I know she wants to ask me something because she's leaning forward in her chair. That's what she does when she wants to have a "serious" conversation. The last time she leaned forward in her chair, she told me that she didn't care if C's were average and that I should be pulling all A's and B's on my report card, even in pre-algebra. But I wasn't in the mood for a serious conversation. I actually had a good day today, and I didn't want her to ruin it. Because when it comes to Mom's serious conversations, they're never serious in a good way.

"So, Molly . . ." Uh-oh. Here it comes. I lick every ounce of ice cream off my spoon so I don't have to answer her. "I want to talk to you about something."

"Yeah?" I scrape the edges of the bowl, making loud scratchy noises.

"I'm staying at Aunt Kathy's for a while." She leans back in her chair, but her gaze doesn't leave me.

"I know. Dad told us." There's no more ice cream left in my bowl; not even one rainbow sprinkle. I put my spoon inside my bowl with a loud clang.

"I might be there for a few weeks."

"A few weeks? Dad said you'd be there for a few days." I crumple my napkin up in a little ball.

"I think some more time away would be best."

"Best for what?" I uncrumple my napkin and start ripping it into little pieces.

"Best for me, actually." Mom takes the napkin out of my hand. "You're making a mess."

"Sorry." I look down at my empty bowl.

"I just want you to know that this has nothing to do with you." Mom reaches across the table and puts her hand on my arm. Her red nail polish clashes with my pink hoodie. "Or your sisters."

"Okay." I nod, pull my arm away, and lean back in the booth so that her hand falls to the table.

"It's just something I need to do for myself right now. You understand." She's not asking me if I understand. She's telling me that I understand, even if I don't. I don't understand how staying at Aunt Kathy's, away from her kids and husband, is best for her. But as with everyone else in our house, it's pointless to argue. She'll lawyer me right out of Clearville Creamery.

"Anyway," she continues, "we could meet for ice cream once a week. Won't that be fun?" She claps her hands together like I'm three years old again.

"Sure," I say.

"That's my girl," Mom says. "And try to help your dad out at home. Eliza and Coco can be a handful, and you know your father can't get out of his own way."

I flinch like she punched me in the stomach. Yeah, I know Dad is a little bit airheaded. But I don't need to hear it from her.

"This sure was fun." Mom stands up and puts her coat on. "Can't wait to do it again."

Mom drives me home, and I wave to her as she pulls out of our driveway. Even with my new rainbow hair, colorful clothes, and popular friends, I feel more invisible than ever.

chapter

* 9 *

COCO'S IN FRONT OF THE TV. AND ELIZA IS IN HER room. At least I'm guessing she's in there since music is blaring from behind the closed door.

I head up to my own room so I can have some privacy. I close the door, throw my backpack onto the chair, and then sit on the edge of my bed. My hands start to sweat, so I quickly add Robert's contact information into my phone before the ink rubs off my palm.

I take a deep breath and press the text icon next to his name. I stare at my phone, hoping something adorable and charming will fly into my fingers. My mind is a complete blank, as if someone went into my head and erased the "vocabulary" part of my brain.

Because I can't think of anything else to write, I decide on the straightforward approach.

Hi. It's Molly. When do you want me to do your hair?

Then I send it before I can change my mind. Two seconds later I feel like I'm going to throw up.

Ugh! I throw myself back onto my bed. That was so lame! *Hi. It's Molly.* He's going to think I'm the biggest dork who ever—

My phone buzzes and I shoot up.

How bout Sat afternoon?

Omigosh omigosh omigosh. My hands are shaking as I read his reply. His reply! He actually wrote back!

Sat afternoon is good.

I delete the period after "good" and replace it with an exclamation point. Or does that sound too anxious? I delete the exclamation point and go back to the period. Much better. I send the text and don't take my eyes off of the phone until he texts back. Which he does immediately.

Gr8. Ur house?

My house? Would that work? Mom won't be here. I could ask Dad, who probably wouldn't care if I had a friend over, but Eliza and Coco would. Only because that friend is a boy who is not Kellan. And they'd totally tell Mom.

Then again, what do I care if they tell Mom? Let them. Maybe if Mom were home being a mom, I could ask her directly.

Yes. 445 Cherry Lane. 2:00

I bite my lip as I wait for his reply.

Sweet!

I flop back down on my bed, this time with a huge grin plastered across my face.

My bedroom door flies open, and the next thing I know, Coco is parked right next to me.

"Whatcha doing?" she asks.

"Nothing."

"Who are you texting?" She leans over to grab my phone.

I pull it away from her. "None of your business. And why didn't you knock?"

Coco shrugs. "What are we doing for dinner?"

"How should I know?" I ask. "Why don't you call Dad?"

"I did." Coco picks at her already-worn-off nail polish. "He didn't answer his phone."

"He never answers," I say. "He'll be home soon."

"I'm hungry. Should I call Mom?" Coco's lower lip is trembling a little, and I'm horrified that she might start to cry. As annoying as she is, sometimes I forget that she's still a little kid. She probably has no idea what's going on between Mom and Dad.

"You can call Mom if you want," I tell her.

Coco wipes her nose with her hand and nods. Her eyes droop and her head hangs low. She looks just like a hound dog.

"Hey," I say, "how about if you and I go downstairs and see if we can find something to make for dinner?"

"Really?" Coco sniffles.

"Yeah. I'm sure we have some pasta or rice or something. How hard can that be to make? If Dad can do it, so can we." I pat her on the knee and stand up.

"Okay!" She stands up too, and her eyes brighten.

She follows me down to the kitchen. I open the pantry and scan the contents. Frosted Flakes. Cheerios. Apple Cinnamon Cheerios. Cocoa Puffs. Froot Loops. I pull boxes and boxes of cereal out and stack them on the counter. I finally find a box of mac and cheese buried in the back.

"Look what I found!" I shake the box. "We could figure out how to make this."

Coco jumps up and down, clapping her hands. "I love mac and cheese."

"Let's see." I look for the directions on the back of the box. "First, we have to boil water."

Coco pinches her lips together. "How do you do that?"

"That's the easy part." I look in the cabinets and find a decent-size pan. "Just fill this halfway with water."

Coco takes the pan to the sink while I continue to read the directions. Looks easy enough.

"We just have to wait for the water to boil," I tell Coco. "And then we'll put the macaroni in."

Coco stares at the pot. "How long until it boils?"

I look at the directions again. "It doesn't say."

We both stare at the water for what feels like hours, until it finally starts to bubble.

"Something's happening!" Coco squeals.

"Let's wait until there are a few more bubbles," I say. "And then we'll put the macaroni in."

Coco's head nods up and down like one of those bobblehead toys. When the water is at a full boil, I slowly pour in the box of macaroni.

"Okay." I stir the noodles with a wooden spoon. "Now we wait a few minutes for it to cook, then we add the sauce and stuff."

Coco clasps her hands together. "This is going to be so yummy!"

We watch the macaroni swim and swirl in the boiling water. After a few minutes I lift a piece out of the pot, blow on it, and pop it in my mouth.

"I think it's ready," I tell Coco, whose eyes follow me as I bring the pot over to the sink and pour the contents into a strainer.

"Is it time to make the sauce?" Coco asks. "That's the best part."

"Yep," I say. "Can you get the milk and butter out of the fridge?"

Coco puts the milk and butter on the counter. I pour the neon orange cheese packet into the pot and add the milk and butter, then mix it all up until, miraculously, it looks just like the mac and cheese Dad makes. I can't wait to see how excited he'll be when he comes home and finds dinner all ready.

"It looks soooooo good." Coco stands on her tiptoes and peers into the pan, which is now bubbling with ooey, gooey cheese.

The garage door makes a rumbling sound, which means that Dad's home.

"Quick," I say to Coco, "set the table."

Coco stares at me. "How do I do that?"

"Just put out some plates and forks," I say. "Oh, and napkins."

Coco pulls four plates out of the cabinet and puts one at each place. She then folds four napkins into triangles and places the forks on top of them. She finishes up with a great big grin just as Dad walks into the kitchen holding Chinese takeout.

"What's this?" He puts the bag on the counter.

"Molly and I made dinner." Coco stands straighter, and her eyes sparkle.

Dad looks at me, then Coco, then back at me again. "Why did you do that?"

The harsh tone of his voice causes my smile to fade. "We thought it would be helpful."

"Or maybe you thought I'd forget about dinner, that without Mom here I can't take care of my own kids?" Dad's lips form a thin straight line as he stares at me.

"No, we just—" I begin to protest, but he interrupts me.

"You should have checked with me first." Dad sighs. "I went out of my way to pick up Chinese."

"That's okay." I force my lips to curl into a smile, even though smiling is the last thing I want to be doing right now. "We'll just save the mac and cheese for tomorrow night."

I put a lid on the pot and move it off of the hot burner.

"Noooo!" Coco whines. "I want mac and cheese tonight!"

"It's not a big deal, Coco." I grit my teeth and stare at her, hoping she'll get the hint. "We'll just save it for tomorrow. You can have it then."

"It's not fair!" Coco stomps her feet. "We worked hard, and it looks yummy."

"Fine. I'm sorry." Dad's shoulders slump. "It was nice of you to make dinner. I guess I'm just not hungry, and I have to get some work done anyway."

He leaves Coco and me there with bags of Chinese food and macaroni and cheese that is getting colder and soggier by the minute.

chapter

* 10 *

I WAKE UP ON SATURDAY FEELING LIKE I MIGHT THROW UP.

My stomach is doing backflips just thinking about the fact that Robert will be here in a few short hours. I need breakfast. Or maybe some fresh air.

After I choke down my Rice Krispies, I hop on my bike and head to the drugstore. I buy the same rainbow hair kit I used on myself. While I'm there, I pick up some markers so I can design the shirts for Team Chocolate Chip Cookies for the Muscular Dystrophy Walk. After that, I swing by Sweet Things, Kellan's favorite bakery, to get him a supersize chocolate chip cookie. I carefully place it inside my backpack, on top of the bag from the drugstore, and then I ride to Kellan's house.

He opens the door before I even knock.

"Hey, Mols." He has a serious case of bed head, with his hair going every which way but the way it's supposed to go. "What are you doing here so early?"

I hold the cookie out to him, and his eyes grow to three times their normal size. "No. Way. Is that what I think it is?"

I nod. "A Sweet Things supersize chocolate chip cookie."

He snatches the cookie from out of my hands and throws his arms around me. "You're the best best friend ever, you know that?"

"Yep," I say.

"And you're just in time because Mom is actually making me wheatgrass juice." Kellan lowers his voice to a whisper. "Did you hear that? I'm having grass for breakfast!"

"Well, now you're having grass *and* a Sweet Things supersize chocolate chip cookie."

"Yessss."

"I gotta go," I say. "I've got to get home and clean up a little."

"Oh, right!" Kellan winks. "Today's the big hair date."

I feel my cheeks heating up. "It's not a date."

"Right." Kellan chuckles. "I can't wait to hear all about it tonight."

My stomach rumbles just thinking about tonight.

Kellan's mom is taking us to Café Ole, the best Mexican food restaurant in the entire universe. She lets us go only a few times a year since she says their food is loaded with fat and salt. That must be what makes it so good.

"I'll give you all the details," I say as I jog back to my bike. "See you at six o'clock!"

Kellan waves from his front porch as he takes a giant bite of his cookie. "See you then," he says, his cheeks filled with chocolaty goodness.

Dad is reading the newspaper at the kitchen table when I get home.

"How was your bike ride?" He puts the paper down and takes a sip of coffee.

"Good." I open the fridge door and grab a bottle of iced tea. "What are you doing today?"

"I have some work to do in the yard," Dad says. "How about you?"

"I'm having a friend over at two o'clock, remember?"

Dad pinches his mouth and furrows his eyebrows like he's trying to remember, but a split second later his face is back to normal. "Oh, that's right."

I swallow down the thickness in my throat. The truth is, I never asked Dad if Robert could come over, but since he's so forgetful, I could say I asked and he wouldn't remember anyway. I shake the guilt out of my head and tell myself it's not that big of a deal. I'm not hiding anything or lying to him.

Not exactly, anyway.

"Where are Eliza and Coco?" The house is unusually quiet.

"Eliza is at a friend's, and Coco is at the movies with Fiona."

"That's good," I say more to myself than to him. Hopefully, they'll be gone all day. It's not that I care if they tell Mom, but I know she'll interrogate me and I don't want to have to explain everything to her.

I spend the next couple hours frantically cleaning my room. I put away my laundry, make my bed, and even drag the vacuum cleaner all the way upstairs. I make sure the bathroom is spotless too, which is no small job, especially since Coco's bath toys are spread out all over the place. I even find a rubber duckie stuffed inside a toilet paper roll that's wedged between the sink and the tub.

I'm almost finished folding the towels when the doorbell rings. I throw the last towel in the linen closet, take a deep breath, and stroll as casually as I can to the door.

When I open it, Robert is on the other side, his skateboard leaning against his leg.

"Hey," I say. And then I stand there scouring my brain for something else to say. My brain has nothing.

"Hey," Robert says. He runs his hand through his hair, which is flopping into his eyes but somehow still looks cool and stylish instead of just plain messy.

We stand there in silence for a minute until Robert asks, "Can I come in, or should we do my hair on the front lawn?"

"Oh, yeah. Of course." A prickly sweat makes its way up my back, and I step aside so he can walk through the door.

Robert Jackson is in my house.

I wish I were on Instagram so I could take a picture of him standing in my foyer. Nobody at school would believe it if I told them.

"I have the hair kit," I tell him.

"Sweet!" Robert beams. "I can't wait to rock rainbow hair."

"Do you want something first? Like a snack?" I lead him into the kitchen.

"Sure. What do you have?"

I open the pantry and pull out a package of Oreos and a bag of chips. Robert takes some of each. Then I fill two glasses with iced tea.

We sit on the stools in front of the kitchen counter.

"So why'd you decide on rainbow hair?" Robert asks between gulps of iced tea.

I shrug. "Just wanted a change, I guess."

"Yeah." Robert nods. "I get that. Change is good."

"Why do you want rainbow hair?" I ask him.

"Because it's super cool," he says. "It's a look that tells people that I'm different, you know? That I don't want to be plain and boring like everyone else."

And even though I'm sitting down, my knees feel weak and my face feels hot. Because Robert Jackson just totally read my mind.

I'm hoping another huge sip of iced tea will bring my cheeks back to their normal color. But my hands must be shaking too much, because instead of bringing the glass to my mouth, it hits my chin and iced tea spills all over my shirt.

I let out a little squeal, and Robert jumps off the stool.

I'm too horrified to move, so I just stand there as iced tea drips down my chin, my neck, and my shirt.

Robert must think this is the funniest thing he's ever seen, because he's cracking up. I'm pretty sure that I'm going to die of embarrassment any minute now.

"Got a towel?" Robert asks when he stops laughing long enough to catch his breath.

I point to the pantry. "Bottom shelf."

Robert pulls a dish towel out and throws it at me. Luckily, I manage to catch it.

"That was epic," he says.

I look at him, expecting to see some form of disgust or judgment on his face, but instead, he just looks relaxed and happy. And if I'm being completely honest, a little adorable.

"Yeah." I give him a weak smile and do my best to dry off my shirt. "Let's hope I'm less of a spaz with the hair coloring."

"No worries," he says. "I trust you completely."

A warmth fills my chest. I'm pretty sure my heart just melted a little.

"So should we get started?" Robert pats me on the back, and the toasty feeling radiates through my body.

"Sure. The supplies are already set up in the bathroom."

"Lead the way," Robert says, and follows me upstairs.

chapter

* 11 *

FOR THE NEXT THIRTY MINUTES ROBERT AND I HARDLY
talk. He's sitting on the edge of the bathtub, and I'm con-
centrating so hard on making sure the colors are perfectly
spaced, with each strand of hair covered. I bite my lip as I
put the final color (bright blue) in the last section of his
hair, which, by the way, is surprisingly soft for a boy's.

"Okay," I say as I place the plastic cap over his head.
"Now you have to sit still for twenty minutes."

I set the alarm on my phone, and Robert stands and
stretches.

"You're supposed to sit still," I say.

"I'll stand still. How's that?"

"I guess that's okay." I glance at the directions. It
doesn't say anything about standing.

"Let's see what's going on here." Robert glances in the mirror. "Whoa. I look like my grandma."

I giggle. "I don't think you'll still look like your grandma after the process is finished."

"I hope not."

I lean against the bathroom door. "Did you ask your parents if you could color your hair?"

"Nah," Robert says. "They pretty much leave me alone when it comes to things like that. Why, did you?"

"No," I say.

"Did your parents care?" Robert sits back down on the edge of the bathtub.

"Not at all," I say, and I'm surprised that the words fly out of my mouth like arrows. Robert must be surprised too, since he raises his eyebrows and looks at me until I say something else.

"They're kind of distracted right now." I look down at the tiled floor.

"Why?" he asks.

"They're kind of in a fight." I kick the tile with my toe.

"Oh, yeah." Robert nods. "My parents used to fight all the time."

My head snaps up. "They used to fight? Not anymore?" I wonder if he can share their secret.

"They got divorced a few years ago."

A sour feeling builds in my stomach and makes its way up to my throat, but I swallow it down before it takes over my entire body. "That stinks."

"Yeah." He's looking in the mirror again. He lifts up the edge of the plastic cap, then puts it back down. "I'm used to it."

I can't imagine getting used to having divorced parents. What if I wind up seeing my mom once a week for ice cream for the rest of my life? Could I actually get used to that? And what about Coco and Eliza? Dad can't handle either of them on his own.

My brain is so far down the divorce what-if that I actually jump when the alarm on my phone goes off.

"Is it time?" Robert looks like a five-year-old on Christmas morning.

"Almost," I say, shaking the divorce thoughts out of my head. "We have to rinse this out."

I have Robert put his head in the sink as I watch the reds and blues and yellows and greens intertwine with one another and swirl down the drain. His hair is lighter than mine, and I can already tell that the color will be more vibrant on him than it is on me.

I turn the water off and towel-dry his hair before I let him look in the mirror. I want it to be perfect before he sees it.

"Okay," I say. "You can look now."

He stands up and stares into the mirror. "Whoa."

He studies himself from different angles, but I can't tell if he likes what he sees.

He finally shifts his gaze from the mirror to me. His green eyes look even greener when up against the array of color on his head.

"It's freakin' fantastic," he says, and then he wraps his arms around me for a hug. The hug lasts for only a fraction of a second, but still.

Robert Jackson hugged me.

"I've been eyeballing this hoodie at the mall," Robert says. "It's, like, neon yellow, and it would totally match my hair. I can't wait to get it tonight."

"That's cool," I say. And I mean it. Because it's amazing what new hair can do to your desire for a new wardrobe.

"You should come," he says.

I blink.

"To the mall," he says, as if I didn't understand what he meant the first time.

"Tonight?" I ask.

"Yeah, Wade and I are meeting Christina and Nina there."

My mind is buzzing, and I wouldn't be surprised if

Robert could actually hear the noise coming out of my ears.

"I'd love to go," I say, without even thinking about it.

"Awesome," he says. "My mom's going to drop me off at seven. We can swing by and get you a little before that."

"Great!"

"Hey." Robert takes one last look in the mirror before we leave the bathroom. "Thanks so much for the hair."

I smile. "It was fun."

I open the front door, and Robert grabs his skateboard. "See you tonight!"

I wave and then close the front door. It's only when I reach into my pocket to check my phone that panic rises in my chest.

There's a text from Kellan.

Can you taste the enchiladas already? Can't wait til dinner!

Dinner.

I'm supposed to go to Café Ole tonight with Kellan.

How did I forget?

I put my head in my hands. I have to tell one of them that I can't make it, but I have no idea which one that will be.

chapter

* 12 *

"HEY, MOLS." KELLAN PICKS UP MY CALL ON THE FIRST ring. "Is your mouth watering yet?"

"That's why I'm calling." I choke the words out. "I don't think I'm going to be able to go tonight."

"You're kidding? Why not?" Kellan sounds equally surprised and disappointed.

"I'm not feeling well." My throat does feel like it's coated with tiny daggers, so I'm not exactly lying.

"That stinks," he says. "I'm really sorry to hear it. Maybe my mom can call Café Ole and see if we can reschedule."

"That would be great," I say, and my body instantly relaxes. If we could do it another night, my problem would be solved.

"Hold on, I'll ask."

I hear voices, but I can't make out what they're saying. Kellan must have put his phone down. After a minute he comes back on.

"Mom said it took two months to get this reservation, so she won't be able to get another one for a while." Kellan's voice sounds flat now, and the daggers in my throat move down into my stomach. I should just tell him I'm feeling better. I should text Robert and tell him I can't make it. But for some reason, the words won't come out of my mouth. So instead, I say nothing, and for the first time in forever, I don't know what to say to Kellan.

"I hope you feel better," he finally says.

"Thanks. I hope you have a good dinner."

"We will. But it won't be as good without you there."

I hang up feeling like maybe I am sick. My head hurts, and my stomach is roiling. But even so, I'm still looking forward to going to the mall. This is my chance to actually make some friends at school, and I won't lie—I'm super excited to spend time with Robert.

So if I made the right decision, why do I feel so horrible?

Robert's mom's car pulls into the driveway a few minutes before seven. I yell to Dad that I'm leaving and run outside.

Robert's in the front seat. He doesn't move to the back when I get in.

Robert introduces me to his mom, who says nothing for the entire drive. In fact, nobody says anything. Robert plays with the buttons on his mom's radio, looking for a song he likes. This continues until we pull into the mall's parking lot ten minutes later.

"Thank you, Mrs. Jackson," I say as I open the back door.

She just nods, then says to Robert, "I'll pick you up here at nine o'clock on the dot. Don't be late."

"Yep," Robert says as he closes the door. As his mom pulls away, I wonder how someone so happy and upbeat can have a mother who's completely the opposite. But then I think of my mother and realize how totally possible it is.

"We're supposed to meet everyone at the food court," he says. "I can't wait to see what they think of my new 'do."

I laugh. "I'm sure they'll love it."

"Right?" Robert's smile takes up his entire face. "It's awesome."

There are a bunch of other kids our age at the mall, and they all stare at us as we walk by. But they're not staring in a bad way. They're nudging each other and pointing and looking at us with big eyes and smiles. They're checking out our hair, and it seems they like it. Maybe we'll start a trend and every kid in Cherry Creek will soon have rainbow hair.

We get to the food court, and Wade, Christina, and Nina are sitting around a table drinking supersize cups of soda and sharing a small order of fries.

"Dude!" Wade yells when he sees us, and Christina and Nina follow his gaze. Nina lets out a little squeal when she sees Robert's hair, and Christina's eyes look like saucers.

"Wow," Nina says as we join them at the table. "Your hair looks so cool!"

"Dude," Wade says again, giving Robert a fist bump. "Nice. But still not as awesome as mine." Wade reaches up and pulls on one of his dreadlocks, which, I have to admit, are pretty wild.

"Did you do his hair?" Christina asks me.

"Yeah." I cross my fingers under the table that she likes it and doesn't think he looks like a pack of Starburst.

"It looks good." She smiles, but her lips are squeezed together like she's trying to hide something stuck in her teeth.

My shoulders relax, and I sit up a little straighter.

"Do you think it would work with my hair?" Nina asks, holding out a section of long, black, shiny hair for me to inspect.

"I don't know," I say. "But if I had your hair, I'd leave it as it is. It's so pretty and shiny."

"Really?" Nina grins. "Thank you."

"Maybe we can just do our tips," Christina tells Nina. "Then the look would be our own. We don't want to copy other people, you know."

Nina looks down at the table and nods. "That's a good idea." But she doesn't seem too excited about it.

We leave the food court and find the store with the neon yellow hoodie that Robert wants. Just like he predicted, it looks perfect next to his new hair.

I follow Christina and Nina to the other side of the store where the girls' clothes are. Everything in here looks like it was custom-made for Eliza.

"Oooohhhhh." Christina picks up a fuzzy silver sweater and drapes it in front of her. "What do you think of this?"

Nina rubs her hands on the sleeve. "It's so soft."

"Let's try it on." Christina hands one to Nina and one to me, and we follow her to the dressing rooms in the back of the store.

I slip the sweater over my head and glance in the mirror. It's tighter than anything I've ever worn before and even more sparkly than the clothes I've been wearing from the bottom of Eliza's closet. I turn to the right and then to the left. I pull the bottom of the sweater down, but it won't go any farther. I debate getting a bigger size.

"Let's see, girls." Christina's voice is singsongy outside of the dressing room. The door next to me opens, and Nina walks out.

Christina looks her up and down. "I don't know. It's okay."

Nina flinches a tiny bit. "It looks really good on you."

"Well, it is my color," Christina agrees.

"Molly, maybe it will look better on you than it does on me," Nina calls through the dressing room door.

I tug at the bottom of the sweater one more time. It still doesn't budge. I take a deep breath and slowly step out of the safety of my private little cube.

"Eeeeep!" Nina claps her hands. "You look adorbs!"

"It doesn't look bad," Christina chimes in, even though she says it like she doesn't want to admit it.

"You know what?" Nina bounces on her toes. "We should all get them! Then we could match."

"But it doesn't really look that good on you." Christina looks at Nina like she's a lost puppy.

Nina shrugs. "That's okay. It will still be fun to match."

Nina pulls Christina in on one side of her and me on the other, so we're standing in a line with our arms around one another, facing the mirror.

"It is pretty cool to match," Christina says.

And she's right. It is.

"Let's do it," Christina declares. "We can all wear them on Monday."

My phone buzzes in my pocket just as I finish paying for the sweater. There goes a month's allowance.

I pull my phone out, and there's a text from Kellan. It's a picture of the most mouthwatering nachos I've ever seen. The chips are slightly browned at the edges, and the orange cheese oozes over the side of the plate. The black beans are perfectly spaced across the top, and small flecks of cilantro are sprinkled above them.

Wish u were here! Feel better.

Ugh. I take a deep breath to try to clear the guilt from my body, but my lungs feel like they're out of air. I've never lied to Kellan, not once in our ten years of friendship.

"Earth to Molly." Christina's waving her hand in front of my face.

"Oh, sorry." I give my head a little shake. "Just wondering which earrings to wear with the sweater."

"I know, right?" Christina says. "I'd say anything silver."

"I agree," I say, and make a mental note to wear silver earrings on Monday.

We all stroll back out into the mall and walk around a

little until Christina puts her arms out, gasps, and points at a mannequin in the window of Windsor.

"That dress would be amazing for my Birthday Bash Brunch." Christina runs up to a dress rack at the front of the store and holds up a sparkly gold dress that seems to change color when it moves.

"Omigod." Nina's hands fly up to her mouth. "It so would."

The Birthday Bash Brunch. Are they actually talking about the Birthday Bash Brunch?

Robert leans forward to whisper in my ear. "Has Christina hinted at inviting you to her famous Birthday Bash yet?"

I shake my head.

"You do know about it, though, right?"

I nod. Of course I know about it. Everyone in the entire state knows about it. She holds it at her parents' country club every year, and it's the talk of the town. Even the adults gossip about it. It's epic. It's legendary. It's also highly selective. Only ten kids get invited.

"Have you been?" I ask him.

"Oh, yeah." Robert closes his eyes and smiles.

"What's it really like?" I ask. I mean, I love brunch, but I'm guessing the reviews are pretty overrated.

Robert smiles. "First of all, the food is to die for. They

have three chocolate fountains—one dark, one milk, and one white chocolate. And an entire buffet filled with desserts, all you can eat."

My stomach rumbles just thinking about it.

"And then," he goes on, "there are the video games. State-of-the-art. And a soundstage to shoot your own music videos."

"Wow," I whisper.

"And the goodie bags?" Robert leans closer to me. "They're filled with the most amazing candy that you can't even get in this country. And there are always gift certificates to stores, restaurants, and stuff like that—one year she had actual fifty-dollar bills in there!"

I glance around to be sure nobody else is listening and then lower my voice. "So she pays people to come to her party?"

Robert laughs. "No way. It's just part of the shindig. Believe me, she doesn't have to pay anyone to go to this party. It's super exclusive, and every year our entire grade waits to see the invitation list."

I've heard all about it, but never in a million years did I think I'd know anyone who actually went.

"It sounds awesome." I sigh, dreaming of chocolate fountains.

"Well, you just might get an invitation." He puts his

arm around my shoulder. *Robert Jackson has his arm around my shoulder.* I zip my jacket up so he can't see my heart beating out of my chest. "You are most definitely in the running now."

I swear if Robert's arm wasn't around me, I would be drifting at least six inches above the floor.

"When do these invitations go out?" I ask.

"It could be any day now. The party's coming up. Sometimes Christina likes to send them out early so everyone gets all excited for weeks, and sometimes she sends them out last minute to keep everyone guessing. You just never know."

I bite my lip.

"Don't worry." Robert squeezes my shoulder. "I'll put in a good word for you."

We walk out of the store, and Robert still has his arm around my shoulder. That's why I don't notice that Kellan and his mom are walking toward us until we are practically right in front of them.

chapter

* 13 *

I ROLL AWAY FROM ROBERT'S GRASP AND DUCK INTO
the nearest store, which happens to be a LensCrafters. I
pretend to be engrossed in a pair of cat-eye glasses with
ruby red frames.

"Uhhh"—Robert is standing beside me—"you wear
glasses?"

My face promptly turns the color of the frames. "Not
really," I mumble.

"This is an eyeglass store." He sweeps his arm across
the shelves of eyewear. "Why are we here?"

I slip the glasses onto my face and pretend to look in
the tiny mirror. "Well, I don't wear glasses now, but my
eyes could get worse at any time." I look over his shoulder at the people strolling by. I don't spot Kellan or

Mrs. Bingham, but they could still be lingering around. I have to buy some time. "I think it's smart to be prepared."

"For when your eyes get bad?" Robert raises an eyebrow.

"Yes." I put the cat-eye glasses back on the shelf and try on a pair of tortoiseshell frames. They don't look too bad.

"You really are a planner," Robert says.

My eyes dart back to the mall. Christina is standing next to Wade and Nina, her arms crossed in front of her chest. She looks annoyed. I scan the crowd, but there's no sign of Kellan.

"You know what?" I walk toward the store's exit. "I'll just come back another time. When my eyes actually start to fail."

Robert throws his hands in the air. "Suit yourself."

I catch up with the rest of our group. "Sorry. I just saw something I might need."

"Well, let's go," Christina says. "I'm totally craving a nonfat caramel latte, and we only have half an hour until our parents come to get us."

"Sorry," I say again, this time under my breath, and follow them to the coffee place.

What is Kellan doing at the mall at this hour? He hates the mall. Plus, he was using his leg braces, which means he wasn't feeling great. Another reason to stay far away from the mall. And then it hits me. Café Ole is in this mall! This is definitely too close for comfort.

Luckily, Christina leads us to a table in the corner. Robert and I order hot chocolate with whipped cream (another thing we have in common!), Christina and Nina order lattes, and Wade orders black coffee, which looks kind of disgusting.

"Did you guys see what Maddy Carter was wearing yesterday?" Christina asks in between sips of her latte.

"Who cares? She's a has-been," Wade says.

"Well, duh." Christina rolls her eyes. "But that's what makes it so ridiculous. She went with her parents to Italy over break, and she came home with all these outfits from Milan. Which would be totally cool if she weren't the one wearing them. Now she just looks like she's trying too hard. Right, Nina?"

Nina nods, but she doesn't take her eyes off of her latte.

"She's a loser," Wade says.

"Omigod." Christina points out toward the mall. "Isn't that the kid who used to go to our school who got crippled or something?"

I know who she's pointing at even before I look up. Sure enough, there's Kellan. Mrs. Bingham is behind him holding a shopping bag.

Nina and I glance at each other for a fraction of a second, but neither of us says anything. I don't expect her to. She hasn't been friends with him in a few years. But I know I should. I should defend Kellan and explain to Christina that he's not "crippled." He has muscular dystrophy. Mrs. Bingham always says that people are much kinder when they're educated. Maybe Christina just doesn't know any better.

But if I open my mouth, Christina might remember that I was actually best friends with him—that I *am* actually best friends with him. My mind races through the possible scenarios:

1. Christina listens carefully as I explain muscular dystrophy. She feels awful for calling Kellan "crippled" and apologizes profusely. Then she calls him over to join us, because, after all, we're best friends.
2. Christina ignores what I say and decides that, despite my cool hair and newfound fashion, I'm still a loser.

Both scenarios are equally bad.

So I keep my mouth shut until he passes by. I spend the rest of the night with my eyes glued to the mall, but I don't see Kellan again.

At nine o'clock we meet Robert's mom in front of Macy's, where she dropped us off. She doesn't say a word to us on the drive to my house. Nobody talks. It's the quietest car ride I've ever experienced.

"Later," Robert says as we pull into my driveway.

"Thanks for the ride," I say.

I'm on the front porch before I spot a gift bag hanging on the door handle. I pull it off and peer inside. There's a card with my name on it.

I kick my shoes off, yell to my dad that I'm home, and take the bag up to my room. I sit on my bed and open the envelope.

Dear Molly,

Sorry you missed tonight! Hope these help you to feel better. I thought of you as soon as I saw them!

Your friend,
Kellan

I take the tissue paper out, and inside is a pair of rainbow-colored Converse sneakers. I slip them on, and they fit perfectly.

MOLLY IN THE MIDDLE

I flop down on my bed and press my palms against my eyes.

I don't deserve a friend like Kellan.

I know what I have to do. I have to tell him the truth.

And I'm going to do it first thing tomorrow morning.

chapter

* 14 *

I WAKE UP WITH WHAT FEELS LIKE A BOWLING BALL IN my stomach.

After sleeping on it, I'm not quite sure I should tell Kellan the truth. I mean, would it do him any good? No. It would just make him feel bad. The only one who would feel better is me, because I wouldn't be carrying around the guilt anymore. So in the interest of Kellan's feelings, I decide not to say anything.

I design the T-shirt for Team Chocolate Chip Cookies instead. And when I'm done, I make real chocolate chip cookies for Kellan.

I pack the cookies in a container and place it in my backpack, along with the shirt design. When I get to Kellan's front door, I take the cookies out even before I ring the bell.

When he opens the door, the first thing he sees is the container of cookies in my outstretched hand.

"Oh, wow," he says. "More cookies! Are all of these for me?"

"Yep," I say, my voice a little too chipper. "Every single one."

"Thank you!" He grabs the container, opens the lid, and takes a whiff. "Oh, man, these smell good."

"And look!" I hand him the shirt design. "For Team Chocolate Chip Cookies."

Kellan takes the sketch from me, a big smile covering his face. "It's us, but in chocolate chip cookie form."

"Yep." I point at the cookie wearing a superhero shirt. "That's you. And the one with rainbow hair is me."

"Looks exactly like us," Kellan says. "If we were chocolate chip cookies!"

"I'm glad you like it," I say. "We'll be the sweetest team at the MD Walk."

"Hey, how are you feeling?" Kellan has a little crease in his forehead, the one he always gets when he's concerned.

"Oh, I'm fine." I wave my hand in front of my face. "Must have been a weird twelve-hour bug."

"You found the gift!" Kellan points to the new shoes on my feet. "We got home late, and I didn't want to wake you. I figured you'd find it this morning."

"Yes, and you didn't have to do that. In fact, you shouldn't have done that." I look down at the shoes, and my voice drops. "I really don't deserve these."

"Don't be ridiculous," Kellan says. "My mom had to get something at the mall after dinner last night. I saw these and knew they'd be perfect for you."

"Thank you," I say softly.

"You're welcome." Kellan leans against the door. "Want to come in?"

"I wish I could," I say. "I've got to babysit Coco today while my dad runs some errands. Eliza's at her friend's house all weekend."

"Your mom still at your aunt's house?"

"Yep," I say. "We have an ice-cream date scheduled for Tuesday."

Kellan rolls his eyes. "That's just weird."

"Hey," I say, trying to change the subject, "want to walk tomorrow?"

"We probably should," Kellan says. "I need the practice."

"Okay, I'll see you after school." Kellan waves from the doorway as I head down the steps of his front porch. I still feel a little guilty for not telling him the truth about last night, but seeing him so happy about the cookies makes me feel mostly okay.

Dad is scrambling around the house when I get home.

"Where's my wallet?" He's checking his jacket pockets, which are coming up empty.

"Have you checked your office desk?" I ask. "That's usually where I see it."

"No, but I'm sure I put it in my jacket this morning." He mumbles something about maybe that was yesterday morning as he heads for his office.

"Here it is," he calls. "I found it."

Coco's perched in her usual spot in front of the television. I grab the remote and click off the power.

"Hey!" Coco yells. "I was watching that."

"Not anymore," I say. "I'm in charge, and we're going to do something outside today."

"You are not in charge." Coco pouts. "Daddy!"

"What is it, Coco?" Dad calls from down the hall.

"Molly's not in charge, right?" She's standing now, with her hands firmly on her hips.

"Yes, she is," Dad calls back. "I have to go grocery shopping."

"Grocery shopping?" Coco crinkles up her nose. "Mommy goes grocery shopping."

"Well, Mommy's not here right now, and we're out of food." Dad gives her a kiss on the forehead. "Listen to Molly while I'm out."

"Don't forget to get Cocoa Puffs," Coco tells Dad.

"It's on my list." Dad shoves a crumpled piece of paper into his pocket. "See you soon."

"Okay, Coco," I say once Dad leaves. "Let's go get some fresh air."

"But it's cold outside," Coco whines.

"No, it isn't! It's beautiful out there." I point to the window. How can she want to sit inside on such an awesome spring day?

"Fine." Coco stomps to the closet for her jacket. "But only for a little while."

I feel immediately more relaxed when we get outside. The sun is strong, and a light breeze sends spring scents whirling through the air.

"It stinks out here." Coco waves her hand in front of her nose.

"No, it doesn't," I say. "It smells like spring."

"It smells like horse poop."

I roll my eyes. Only Coco would mistake the smell of freshly mowed grass for horse poop.

"What are we supposed to do out here?" Coco looks around like she's landed on an alien planet.

"Let's go on the swings," I suggest.

"That's boring." Coco kicks a clump of grass with her foot.

"We could climb trees," I say.

Coco shrugs, which is better than an outright no.

"See that one over there?" I point to a big oak toward the back of our property. "That was my favorite one when I was your age."

"You climbed that when you were my age?" Coco looks from me to the tree and back again.

"Sure," I say. "It's not hard."

"It looks hard." She squints her eyes at the tree, as if it just personally offended her.

"Come on." I start walking across the yard. "I'll show you."

Coco follows. I pick up the pace a bit, hoping that maybe she'll actually run. Eight-year-olds should run in the grass and climb trees. That's what I did when I was eight. And even though Eliza is four years older than me, we did all that stuff together when we were kids. I'm not sure what happened to Coco.

"Okay," I begin as we reach the oak. "First, grab on to this branch."

Coco stands on her tiptoes and barely reaches the branch. It's funny how easy it is for me now. The last time I did this it seemed much higher up.

"Good!" I say as she gets a strong hold on it. "Now pull yourself up like this." I swing my legs up and over the branch, so I'm hanging upside down.

"I can't do it," Coco says after a few tries. "It's too high."

"Let me help you." I jump down and give her a boost. Once she's higher up, she grabs on to the branch and pulls her feet up, just like I instructed.

"I did it!" she yells. She's hanging upside down, and the look of fear that shaded her face a minute ago is replaced with joy.

"Good job," I say. "Now pull yourself up so you're sitting on the branch."

Coco tries to pull herself up, but she just doesn't have the strength. I guess this kind of stuff takes practice.

"I can't do it." She's huffing and puffing, but she can't lift her body high enough.

I stand underneath her and give her a shove. "Now, quick, pull yourself up!"

She does what I say, and amazingly enough, it works. She's now sitting on the branch.

"I did it! I did it!" Her voice is high and excited.

"You did it!" I say. "That's great."

"This is fun. I want to go higher!"

"Okay, okay." I laugh. "Now you have to stand up on the branch you're sitting on and hold on to the trunk."

Slowly, Coco shifts her feet onto the branch and stands. She wraps her arms around the tree trunk like her life depends on it.

"Now let go with one hand and grab the next branch."

Coco shakes her head. "I can't let go."

"Yes, you can," I say. "Just do one hand at a time."

"It's too high," Coco says. "I'm gonna fall."

"You'll be fine. Just don't look down."

And that's when Coco looks down.

"I don't want to be up here anymore!" Her eyes bubble with tears.

"But you're so close," I tell her.

"No." She shakes her head violently back and forth. "I want to come down."

I sigh. "Okay. You have to sit down again first. Slide back down onto your butt."

Still clinging to the tree trunk, Coco slides down so that she's crouched on the branch.

"Now let go of the tree, sit down, and hold on to the branch."

"I can't let go!" Her lower lip is trembling.

"You have to," I tell her. "It's the only way to get down. Just focus and do it slowly. One hand and then the other."

"I can't!" She's trembling all over now.

"Coco, you have to calm down. You can't do this if you're freaking out."

"I can't calm down," she yells. "Just get me off of here!"

"You have to listen to what I say." I talk slowly and keep my voice extra calm, hoping it will rub off on her. "Let go of the trunk and put your hand on the branches. But do it slowly."

"Come get me!" Coco screams.

"I can't come get you," I tell her, my voice rising more than I'd like it to. "The branch won't hold both of us."

"I can't do it!" She's got her arms wrapped so tightly around the tree trunk that I can barely tell where the bark ends and her jacket begins.

"Just let go of—"

And just like that, she lets go.

"No, slowly—" I yell, but it's too late. Her arms miss the branch, and she topples to the ground below.

chapter

* 15 *

COCO'S FACE IS COMPLETELY BLANK FOR A FRACTION of a second. And then the screaming begins.

I'm at her side in a flash. "Where does it hurt?" I can barely hear myself over her cries and the drumming of my own pulse in my ears.

"My arm!" Coco clutches her wrist as she writhes on the ground. I reach for her arm, but she screams even louder. "Don't touch it!"

My brain freezes, kind of like my laptop sometimes does when it's overloaded. There's too much to process, and I don't know what to do next. I slump down beside Coco in the grass, rubbing her back as she screeches.

I have to get to a phone. I have to call someone who will know what to do.

I take a deep breath. "Can you stand up?"

"Nooooooo!" Coco answers in between sobs.

"Do your legs hurt?"

"I." Sob. "Don't." Sob. "Know." Sob.

"How about if you try to stand up? I need to get to a phone, and I don't want to leave you here by yourself." I get to my feet, hoping she'll follow my lead.

"I can't," Coco says. But she didn't even try.

"Come on, Coco." My jaw clenches. "You have to give it a shot."

"I can't," she wails.

"We'll go inside, and I'll call Dad while you watch TV."

This gets her attention. She stops crying long enough to roll over onto her side.

"That's it," I tell her, gently holding her under the arm that doesn't hurt. "You can do this."

Coco slowly gets to her feet, tears still pouring out of her eyes. Her face is covered with dirt, but at least I don't see any blood.

"It hurts," she says. "Bad."

"I know." I move as fast as I can across the backyard, practically dragging Coco along with me. When we finally get inside, I set her gently on the couch and place the remote control in her good hand. She's still crying, but not nearly as hard as before. "I'll be right back. I'm going to call Dad."

She nods and flips the channel to her favorite cartoon.

I grab the house phone, since my cell phone is still in my room, and dial Dad's number. It goes straight to voice mail. Of course.

"Ummm, Dad?" I begin. "It's Molly. There's been a little accident, and Coco is hurt. It's her arm. Please call me back."

I stand over the phone for fifteen minutes, willing it to ring. Coco's cries get louder, and I do what I should have done in the first place.

I call Mom.

Mom answers immediately. "What is it, Molly? I'm about to go into a spin class."

"Oh." I swallow. "It's just that . . ."

"Molly, is something wrong?" Mom's voice is more high-pitched than usual.

"It's Coco," I blurt out. "She's hurt."

"How badly?" Mom never panics in a crisis. She just gets right to the point.

"I don't know. Her arm hurts. She fell out of a tree."

Silence.

"Where's your father?" She's switched to lawyer voice. Not good.

"Grocery shopping. I was babysitting. I tried calling him but—"

"I'm on my way." And then she hangs up.

I rush back to Coco, whose sobs are starting to ramp up again. "Mom's on her way."

For some reason, this makes Coco cry harder, and the pressure behind my own eyes builds. But I can't cry. I have to hold it together for Coco.

"Can I get you anything? Some juice, maybe? A cookie?"

Coco shakes her head. It must be bad if she's turning down cookies. She's still holding her right wrist, so I can't get a good look at it.

I spend the next fifteen minutes sitting next to Coco watching cartoons, although it's hard to hear over her sobs and groans.

"It really hurts." She says this every thirty seconds or so, and I nod sympathetically each time.

"Molly?" Mom's voice echoes from the front door.

"In here," I call out.

Mom's sneakers squeak down the hallway until she reaches the rug in the living room. She's dressed for her weekend spin class. Black bike shorts. A white tank top. She stops to survey the situation before walking over to lean down next to Coco.

"Mommy!" Coco wipes her face with her good hand. "My arm hurts. Badly."

"Let me see." I move off the couch and stand to the side, so Mom can do her Mom thing. Coco screams when Mom touches her wrist.

Mom stands up, pursing her lips. "It needs an X-ray."

Coco cries even louder at that. "What's that? Will it hurt?"

"It's just something that will help a doctor see your bones. It doesn't hurt, Coco. But we do have to go to the hospital."

The garage door rumbles, and Dad comes trudging up the steps carrying a bunch of grocery bags. "Karen, I saw your car. What are you doing here?" His eyes are bright, like he's happy to see her. But when he sees Coco, his entire face droops. "What happened?"

"I don't know, Paul," Mom says. "You tell me."

Dad looks at me.

"I was teaching Coco to climb a tree, and she fell." I blink back the tears that are ready to spring from my eyes.

"I hurt my arm," Coco adds in between hiccups.

Dad drops the grocery bags and joins Coco on the couch. "Oh no, honey. Let me see."

"I already looked at it." Mom crosses her arms. "She needs an X-ray."

"I'll take her," Dad says.

"I'll take her," Mom says, her voice clipped. "I've already missed my spin class today."

"I'll go with you," Dad says.

"No." Mom glares at Dad. "You've already done enough."

"What's that supposed to mean?" Dad throws his arms in the air.

"Maybe if you were watching them—"

"Watching them?" Dad interrupts. "Molly was baby-sitting. You've left Molly alone with Coco a million times!"

"And nothing like this ever happened on my watch." Mom's lawyer voice.

"Nothing like this happens on your watch because it's hardly ever your watch. You don't spend any time at home!" Dad's face is bright red, and the vein in his forehead is sticking out.

"I'm never home? You're never home!" Now Mom's raising her voice too. I'm not sure which is worse. When Mom yells or when she doesn't.

Coco starts crying even louder now, not that I can blame her.

Mom squeezes her eyes shut and takes a deep breath. "We'll discuss this later. I'm taking Coco to the hospital."

And as both of them help Coco up from the couch, I disappear into my room.

Nobody even notices.

chapter

* 16 *

A FEW HOURS LATER MOM BRINGS COCO HOME. SHE'S got a neon pink cast on her right arm.

"I told you we should have stayed inside," she tells me the second she sees me.

"Remember what the doctor told you," Mom says to Coco. "You have to wrap your cast in a plastic bag when—"

"I know, I know." Coco bounces over to the couch, where she finds the remote control.

"Coco!" Mom's voice is sharp, and Coco knows she means business. She drops the remote and heads back toward Mom. "You have to listen. You can't count on anyone else to do this for you." She glares at Dad.

"I can handle it, Karen."

Mom just ignores him. "Coco, you have to wear a plastic

bag while taking a bath. And even if it gets itchy, don't put anything inside your cast. It could get stuck there."

"Okay, okay," Coco says, and then peeks toward the kitchen. "I'm hungry."

"I'll make you a sandwich," Dad says, then adds, under his breath, "if your mother thinks I'm capable enough."

"So, Coco, I'll see you tomorrow for our ice-cream date." Mom gives her a peck on the cheek.

"Yay! Ice cream." Coco fist pumps her good arm.

"And, Molly"—Mom turns to me—"I'll see you on Tuesday."

I nod. She gives me a quick hug and leaves without saying anything to Dad.

When Eliza gets home after dinner, Coco recaps the entire story, with some added exaggeration in there for shock value.

"Molly made me climb to the top of the tree, and then she told me to jump down . . ."

I roll my eyes. This is the tenth time I've heard this story. She told Dad, and then she called every single friend she has to tell them what a horrible sister/babysitter I am.

"Did Mom freak?" Eliza asks me when we're alone in the kitchen. "I mean, you know, in her Mom way."

I know exactly what she means. Our mother doesn't freak out the way other mothers do. She doesn't yell or scream or stamp her feet. In fact, Mom's way of freaking out is pretty much the opposite of all that. She turns to stone. Her voice gets cold, and her edges get sharp. She becomes an angry statue.

"Yep, pretty much." I fall onto a stool at the counter.

Eliza nods. "That sucks."

"She was really mad at Dad."

"She's always mad at Dad," Eliza says, grabbing an iced tea from the fridge.

"She blamed him." I look down at my feet, which are hanging about six inches above the floor. Seeing them like that makes me feel small.

"She always blames him." Eliza takes a big swig of iced tea, then wipes her mouth with the back of her hand.

"But it was my fault." I practically whisper this, like I'm confessing a deep, dark secret.

Eliza puts her bottle of tea on the counter. "It wasn't your fault."

I snap my head up to look at her. I didn't even think she heard me.

"Yes, it was," I say, swallowing the lump that's growing in my throat. "I made her go outside. I told her to climb the tree."

"So what?" Eliza looks straight at me. "That's what kids are supposed to do."

"But if I didn't do that, Coco wouldn't have broken her arm, and Mom wouldn't have gotten mad at Dad, and—"

"Coco should know how to climb a tree. Mom and Dad should have taught her. Or at least they should have made her go outside once in a while. Instead, they just let her do whatever she wants. You know why?"

I shake my head.

"Because it's easier."

I chew on my lower lip as I think about this. It's true they let Coco watch TV and play video games and eat whatever she wants whenever she wants to do it. But I never actually thought about why.

"Listen, Molly." Eliza sits down on the stool next to mine. "I had to figure this out for myself, but it's the truth. Mom and Dad aren't great parents."

I blink, not sure I heard what I think I heard. "What?"

"They're kind of selfish."

My mouth opens, but no words come out. I don't know what to say to this. I've always known my parents are busy and distracted, but I never thought of them as *selfish*.

"Think about it," Eliza says as she slides off her stool and grabs her bottle of iced tea. "I'm going up to my room."

I sit there, swinging my feet from the stool, as Eliza's

words bounce off my brain. My parents aren't bad parents. That's just Eliza being overdramatic. Bad parents hurt their kids and forget to feed them and don't buy them clothes. Mom takes us shopping all the time. And Dad always picks up takeout. I mean, sure, maybe they're not like Mrs. Bingham, but she's an exceptionally good parent. My parents are . . . My mind searches for the right word. And I find it immediately.

Average.

Just like me.

chapter

* 17 *

THE NEXT WEEK GOES BY IN A BLUR, LIKE THIS NEW
life of mine is only a dream. On Monday, as planned,
Christina, Nina, and I wear our new matching sweaters,
and I can tell that practically the entire seventh grade looks
at me differently because of it. Because of one piece of
clothing.

On Tuesday, Mom and I have another ice-cream date,
but it's about as fun as our first one was. I go by Kellan's
house most afternoons like always, but a lot of my time is
being taken up by helping Coco do just about everything.
Without her right hand, she has trouble getting dressed,
she can't tie her shoes, and she can barely even feed herself. So I've been feeling like her mother, especially with
Mom not at home. I actually feel bad for Coco, and it

makes me question Mom's "mom-ness" even more. She should be here.

I'm actually happy when Monday rolls around, and I find Nina at my locker when I get to school. Surprisingly, she's alone. I rarely see her without Christina.

"OMG, Molly, that skirt is adorbs!" Nina looks even happier than she usually does.

"Oh, thanks." I look down at the skirt that was shoved in the bottom of one of Eliza's bins. It's purple and layered, and it shimmies whenever I move.

"So, I've been meaning to ask you." Nina smiles sheepishly. "How's Kellan? I mean, you're still friends with him, right?"

"Oh, yeah." This question catches me off guard. Even though we were all friends when we were kids, Nina hasn't even seen Kellan since fifth grade. "He's—he's good. I mean, he's doing okay."

Nina sighs, as if she's relieved to hear this. "I think about him sometimes. I wonder how he's doing."

I raise my eyebrows. "Oh, yeah?"

"Yeah." Nina nods. "I'm glad to hear he's doing okay. He was always so—"

"Hi, girls." Christina slides in behind Nina. "Fab skirt, Molly. Whatcha talking about?"

"Oh, nothing." Nina's face turns crimson, and she

waves her hand in front of it, as if she's trying to erase the words that are lingering there. "Just told Molly I love her skirt too."

Christina smiles, her bright pink lip gloss shimmering under the florescent lights of the hallway.

The warning bell rings, and Christina's smile instantly fades. "Ugh. Littman's class first."

I don't mind Mrs. Littman, but I know a lot of the other kids don't like her. She is pretty strict. But as long as you pay attention, she's a fair teacher. I pull my language arts book out of my locker, and the three of us walk to class, chattering away as if we've been friends forever.

Robert's already there when we walk in, throwing crumpled-up paper balls at Wade, who catches them, scrunches them into a tighter ball, and hurls them back. Clearly, Mrs. Littman has stepped out of the room.

"Molly!" Robert smiles at me as he dodges Wade's latest throw. "How goes it?"

"Hi, Robert," I say. I slide into my desk.

"Where's Mrs. Littman?" Nina's eyes dart around the room.

"Who knows?" Robert says, lobbing another paper ball at Wade.

"Who cares?" Christina says, and picks up one of Wade's discarded clumps of paper and throws it at Robert.

"What is going on in here?" Mrs. Littman's voice sounds like nails on a chalkboard, and the entire class freezes. "This is not the kind of behavior I expect from you when I have to step out of the classroom."

"Mr. Jackson, Mr. Barber, and Ms. Golden, pick up that mess, and please make an appointment to see me after school."

Robert and Wade do as they're told, but Christina protests. "Sorry, Mrs. Littman, but I have a meeting after school that I can't miss."

"Well, you'll miss it today."

"I don't think you understand." Christina puts her hands on her hips. "I can't miss it. It's with the caterers at my parents' country club. They're very busy, and we've had this meeting on the calendar for months."

"I don't care if it's with the queen of England, Ms. Golden. I expect you to see me today after school. We're going to have a little lesson on respect and how to behave properly in class."

"But—" Christina begins.

"Take a seat, Ms. Golden. This conversation is over."

Christina stomps over to her desk and hurls herself into her chair. She immediately crosses her arms in front of her, not even bothering to take out her textbook. I cringe.

"Turn to page eighty-three, please," Mrs. Littman

says. She glances at Christina for what feels like hours, until she finally—and dramatically—pulls her book out of her backpack.

When the bell rings and we're in the hallway, Christina pulls Nina, Wade, Robert, and me into a corner. "This is unacceptable. We have to do something."

"It's no big thing," Wade says. "We'll just meet with her after school, apologize, she'll give us a lecture, and then we'll be out of there. It's not like this is the first time for us." Wade points to Robert, who grins.

"Wade's right. It takes less than two minutes, and it makes Littman feel superior."

"I don't care. She's going to pay for this," Christina says. "And you guys are going to help me come up with a plan."

"A plan?" Nina asks, her nose wrinkled.

"Yes, to get her off my case. And to get back at her for being such a crank." Christina squares her shoulders and looks from Nina, to me, to Wade, and then to Robert. Nobody says anything. "Look, I have a very important meeting with the caterer today. To talk about my Birthday Bash Brunch. I'm sure you all want to help me out with this, right?"

"Well, yeah," Robert says. "But you don't want to overreact—"

Christina puts her hands on her hips. "I think you'd

agree, Robert, especially since you've been on the guest list, that my Birthday Bash is *the* party of the year. We can't have anything ruin it. Especially not that hag, Littman."

Robert nods. "Yeah, you're right. I'm in." He puts his fist into the middle of our circle.

"Me too." Wade adds his fist to Robert's.

Nina and I glance quickly at each other. Nina's eyes are wild, like she's been trapped in a cage.

"Well?" Christina says. "Are you guys in?"

Nina nods ever so slightly and slowly adds her fist to the ones in the circle.

I look around at this tight little group, the only one I've ever been a part of, and swallow hard.

"I'm in too."

Christina adds her fist to mine, and we stand there in unison, ready to fight for one another. And even though there's an uncomfortable tug at my stomach, I smile.

Because I finally belong somewhere.

chapter

* 18 *

BY NOON I'M FEELING WIPED OUT FOR SOME REASON. I
swing by the cafeteria to buy a pack of cookies (one for me
and one I'll save for Kellan), and then, instead of going
to lunch, I head to the library. I haven't had lunch in the
library for a while, and I'm surprised to find that I sort
of miss it. The same kids who always eat in the library are
there, and I find their presence comforting. It's nice to
know that some things, at least, don't change.

I snap a picture of Kellan's cookie with my phone and
text it to him.

I'm saving this for u.

I wait for his reply, which comes within seconds.

U r awesome! :)

A smile spreads across my entire face. There's nothing

better in the world than a happy text from your best friend.

I'm in my last period class (Spanish) when someone knocks on the classroom door.

"Entrar!" Senora Gonzalez says.

Christina opens the door and steps inside our class-room. "Hi, Senora Gonzalez. Mrs. Littman asked to see Molly."

Why does Mrs. Littman want to see me? But when I look up at Christina, she just winks.

Senora Gonzalez tilts her head to the side. *"En Español, por favor."*

Christina rolls her eyes. "Um. Señora Littman . . . um . . . um . . . ummm . . ."

"Quiere ver," Señora Gonzalez prods her, thank goodness.

"Yeah, that," Christina says. *"Quiere ver* Molly."

"Ve, Molly. *Hasta mañana."* Señora Gonzalez gives me a wave.

I throw my Spanish notebook into my backpack, sling my backpack over my shoulder, and follow Christina into the hallway.

"What's going on?" I ask. "Why does Mrs. Littman want to see me?"

"She doesn't." Christina saunters down the hallway, her blond bob swooshing back and forth. "It's all part of the plan."

"The plan?" I practically have to jog to keep up with her.

"Yes, the plan to let me keep my appointment with the caterer today. Robert, Wade, and I came up with one during math."

She starts to slow down as we approach Mrs. Littman's classroom, and she stops just shy of the door. "Here's the deal." Christina looks around to be sure nobody's listening, but we're the only ones in the hallway. "You, Wade, and Robert are going to go in there as soon as the bell rings. When she asks why you're there, look confused and tell her that she told you to see her after class."

"But she told *you* to see her after class, not me," I say.

"That's what she thinks," Christina huffs. "But we're going to convince her that she's wrong."

I open my mouth to tell her that we'll never get away with it, but the bell rings. The door to Mrs. Littman's class flings opens, and kids come pouring out. The hallway is suddenly packed with people scrambling to leave for the day. The sudden burst of noise is overwhelming, which is why I jump when Robert taps me on the shoulder.

"Ready for Plan Make Littman Think She's Crazy?"

"I was just explaining the plan to her, but she's not completely on board." Christina rolls her eyes when she says this, and I want to remind her that there are holes in her plan.

"We're going to make Littman think that she asked Wade, me, and you to stay after school," Robert says.

"I know, but how are we going to do that?" I ask.

"We're just going to walk in like you're supposed to be there. And if she questions us, we'll look all confused."

"Yes, but what if she asks the rest of the class tomorrow morning? We'll get in even bigger trouble."

"We've got that covered." Christina smirks. "I already told everyone in the class to go along with it."

"How do you know they will?" I feel a little nauseous, picturing the look that would appear on my mother's face if Mrs. Littman called her in for an impromptu conference.

"Please." Christina waves her hand in front of me. "It's Birthday Bash season. Everyone wants to be on my good side right now."

As the last student leaves Mrs. Littman's classroom, Wade pats Robert on the back. "Let's do this."

"Good luck," Christina whispers before sauntering down the hallway. "I'm counting on you."

Before I can tell them that I don't want to do this, that it's lying to a teacher—and that there's no way Mrs. Littman will fall for it—my legs, which seem to have a mind of their own, follow Robert and Wade into the classroom.

"We're here, Mrs. Littman," Wade says. "As you instructed."

Mrs. Littman looks up from the papers on her desk. "Where's Ms. Golden?"

Robert shrugs. "I have no idea."

"And why is Ms. Mahoney here?" Mrs. Littman raises her eyebrows at me.

"You asked to see us," Robert says.

"I asked to see you two boys"—Mrs. Littman nods to Robert and Wade—"and Ms. Golden."

"I thought you wanted to see the three of us," Robert says, and Wade nods a little too enthusiastically.

"No. I definitely asked to see Ms. Golden." Mrs. Littman turns her gaze to me. "Why are you here, Ms. Mahoney?"

It feels like all the air gets sucked out of the room at that very moment. I take a deep breath in and try to fill my lungs back up before speaking.

"You asked me to see you after school." I can't look her in the eyes, so I stare at the mole on her right cheek instead.

"I asked to see Ms. Golden after school." Mrs. Littman's stare is burning a hole into my head, and I'm pretty sure she can see right inside it.

I square my shoulders and stand up as straight as I can. "No, it was definitely me."

Mrs. Littman's brow furrows for a split second, and Robert takes that opportunity to steer the conversation away from me.

"We shouldn't have been goofing around in class. We're really sorry about that."

"Yeah, we're really sorry," Wade echoes.

"Mmm-hmm." Mrs. Littman leans back in her chair and looks at Robert, then Wade, then me. "How about if you three help me clean up this room?"

"We're on it, Mrs. Littman," Robert says, giving her his best and brightest smile.

After we pick up the papers on the floor, water all of Mrs. Littman's plants, and put the chairs on top of the desks, Mrs. Littman dismisses us. Well, she dismisses Robert and Wade.

"Ms. Mahoney, can I talk to you for a minute?"

Robert gives me a nod and a thumbs-up as he heads out the door. "I'll wait for you in the hallway," he whispers.

I force my feet to walk in the direction of Mrs. Littman's desk. All I want to do is run out of this room, but I have to see this through. I have to play my part in Christina's plan or risk going back to being alone and invisible. And I refuse to do that again.

"Yes, Mrs. Littman?" I'm standing next to her desk, playing with a loose thread hanging from my sweater.

Mrs. Littman gets up from her chair and moves to the front of her desk so she's right next to me.

"You're a good kid, Molly," she begins. I swallow hard, because she never, ever calls anybody by their first name. It makes her sound like a real person instead of just my old, cranky language arts teacher. "I'd hate to see you hanging out with the wrong crowd."

I purse my lips. "The wrong crowd?"

"I've been teaching for a long time." Mrs. Littman gives a little chuckle. "A long time. I've seen all kinds of kids, and I have a pretty good idea of who they are to their cores."

She's looking at me as if she's waiting for me to respond. But I don't know what to say.

"Sometimes good kids make bad decisions," she says. "But ultimately, your choices determine your actions, and your actions determine who you are. If you make good choices, your actions will reflect that. Does that make sense?"

I know she's trying to tell me that she thinks I made a bad decision, covering for Christina. She knows she asked Christina to see her after school and not me. Of course she knows. Mrs. Littman may be boring and old and strict, but she's not stupid. I can't admit any of this to her, so I just nod and hope she'll let me go.

Mrs. Littman takes a deep breath. "Being popular seems important now, Molly, I get that. But believe me when I tell you, when you grow up and become an adult, you won't care whether or not you were popular in middle school. It just won't matter at all. What will matter, though, is that you maintain your integrity. Just remember that."

I nod again, even though she clearly doesn't understand. Middle school was probably a hundred years ago for
her, and she's obviously forgotten what it was like.

Mrs. Littman sighs. "You can go home now, Molly."

"Okay, thank you," I say, and I walk as fast as I can
toward the door. I close it behind me and let out the biggest breath I've ever held. Robert is leaning against the
lockers, and he gives me a huge grin when he sees me.

"You okay?" he asks.

"Yeah." I roll my shoulders, not realizing how stiff
they were when I was talking to Mrs. Littman. "I didn't tell
her anything."

"Good," Robert says. "I was afraid she'd try to corner
you into telling the truth."

I'm not sure what Mrs. Littman was trying to do. I'm
just thankful it's over with.

"Well, this should secure your spot on the guest list for
Christina's Birthday Bash," Robert says.

"You think so?"

"Probably. You took one for the team." He puts his
fist out, and I bump his fist with mine.

All I've ever wanted is to be part of something—part of
a team. And now I am. So as I walk out of school, Robert
by my side, I wonder why I feel like I've been kicked in the
stomach.

chapter

* 19 *

KELLAN SMILES WHEN HE OPENS THE FRONT DOOR.

"Ready for a practice walk?" I hold out the open pack of cookies I bought for us at lunch and brush any thoughts of school today out of my mind. This afternoon is all about Kellan.

"You are the best." Kellan takes the cookie out of the package and shoves the entire thing into his mouth.

"Be back soon, Mom," Kellan calls. But before he can walk out the door, Mrs. Bingham is by his side.

"You're sure you're up for this?" She has her eyebrows raised, like she's doubting that he'll tell her the truth.

"Mom, I'm fine." Kellan kisses her on the cheek. "We won't be long."

Mrs. Bingham pauses for a few seconds, then finally nods her head. "Have fun. And come back if you're not feeling well. Molly, do you have your phone?"

"Yep." I pat my pocket.

"Call me if you need a ride, okay?"

"Sure thing, Mrs. Bingham."

"Bye, Mom." Kellan rolls his eyes and shuts the front door behind us.

We take the same route as always, but we're going slower than usual. Kellan's looking weak today.

"So, how are you feeling?" I keep my voice as light as possible, as if I'm just making casual conversation.

"Oh no," Kellan says. "My mom got to you."

"Not really," I say. "I mean, she's always like that."

Kellan laughs. "That's the truth."

"But really, you feeling okay?"

"Meh," he says. "Been better, been worse."

"Is physical therapy helping much?" I keep my pace slow and steady to match his.

"It's hard to say," he answers. "Maybe I'd feel worse if I didn't have it."

"And how's the green tea therapy?"

Kellan grimaces. "I'm sorry, but that stuff is nasty."

I giggle. "Try adding honey."

Kellan's lip curls. "Still sounds gross."

By the time we arrive at our bench, it's obvious that Kellan wants to sit down, so I sit first.

"Thanks, Mols." Kellan rubs his legs. "I guess I'm just tired."

"That makes two of us," I say. I think about telling him what happened at school today but decide against it. Kellan doesn't need to hear any of my silly drama right now. Plus, if I'm being honest, I don't want to tell him that I lied to Mrs. Littman.

"You know the worst part?" Kellan sighs. "I can't even tell my mom how bad I'm feeling."

"Seriously?" I ask. "You always tell your mom everything."

"I know." He throws up his arms. "That's why this is so hard. But if I tell her, there's no way she'd let me go back to school."

"Maybe that's not such a bad thing," I say. The minute the words leave my mouth, though, they hang in the air like a pack of wasps, ready to sting.

"You said school was fun these days." Kellan furrows his eyebrows, obviously confused by my seemingly sudden change of heart.

"Parts of it are fun," I say. "Parts aren't."

"That's good enough for me, Mols." Kellan leans

back on the bench and closes his eyes. "I could use a little bit of fun in my life."

We sit in silence for a few minutes, but it's the best kind of silence. I'm not wondering what he's thinking, because I know. I always know. Kellan is the best at sharing his feelings. A pang pulls at my stomach because, these days, I'm not so sure that I'm being as honest with him as he's being with me.

"Can I tell you something else?" Kellan looks up at me, a small frown covering his face.

"Of course."

Kellan sits forward on the bench, his elbows resting on his legs. "I'm afraid I won't be able to finish the walk."

"Yes, you will," I say. "I know you will."

"But what if I can't?"

"You can. And you will."

"But what if I can't, Mols?"

My brain is spinning because the thought has never crossed my mind. Of course Kellan will finish the walk. That's why we've been practicing for months.

"I guess I figured if I could do this walk, then there's a chance I could beat this, you know? If I can do this, then I could handle school, and if I could do that, then I could handle the next challenge that comes my way," Kellan says.

"You can handle anything, Kels." I put my hand on his. "I know you can."

"But what if I can't? What if I literally can't put one foot in front of the other?"

"I'll be there to help you." I squeeze his hand. "I'll push you in the wheelchair. I'll carry you on my back. Whatever it takes. We'll do it together."

Neither of us says anything else. We just sit there together, on the bench, holding hands. But the thing is, I'm scared. I've never heard Kellan talk this way. He's always so positive. If Kellan loses hope, then the whole world is doomed.

The next day is ice-cream day. Mom picks me up from school, and we take the short drive to Clearville Creamery.

We settle in, me with my ice-cream sundae and Mom with her plain black coffee. I swirl my spoon around in my bowl, churning together the vanilla ice cream, chocolate sauce, and rainbow sprinkles. Once everything is all mixed together, I dip my spoon in and out, but I don't actually eat any of it.

"Something on your mind, Molly?" Mom sips her coffee.

I debate telling her everything. I'm worried that even though I lied to Mrs. Littman, Christina still won't invite me to her Birthday Bash. I'm worried that Robert won't like me anymore if I don't get invited to Christina's Birthday Bash. I'm worried that Dad doesn't know how to function without Mom there telling him what to do. I'm worried that Kellan is losing hope, and most of all, I'm worried that I don't know how to fix any of these things.

Since I can't talk to Kellan about these things, and since Mom asked, I decide to let loose. "I guess there is—"

I'm interrupted by Mom's cell phone.

"Hold that thought." Mom fishes around in her purse and pulls out her phone. She answers it, then holds one finger up to me as she takes the call outside. I dip my spoon into my sundae, which is quickly turning into a gooey puddle of mush, but I can't bring myself to eat. It feels like there's a rubber band wrapped around my stomach, and food—even ice cream—looks completely unappealing.

"I'm sorry, Molly." Mom walks toward our table, her heels click-clacking on the tile floor. "That's work. I have to go."

"Oh," I say, standing up and grabbing my jacket off the back of my chair.

"It's a potential client I've been chasing for months. He's finally willing to talk to me, and apparently, it's now or never. You understand."

I don't understand. I was just about to tell her what's

going on in my life, and she completely forgot about that as soon as the phone rang. Then I remember what Eliza told me—that Mom and Dad are self-absorbed—and my heart sinks into my stomach as I realize that she's right. But how can I tell Mom this? She doesn't want to hear it now, and it wouldn't matter anyway.

"Rain check?" Mom says to me as we get into her car.

"Sure, Mom," I say, but I know there won't be a rain check. Mom's schedule is written in stone and planned for weeks in advance. I wait for her to ask me what I was going to say before her phone rang, but she doesn't. She pulls into our driveway, gives me a kiss on the cheek, and tells me to have a nice night. Then she hightails it out of our street, clearly breaking the speed limit as she goes.

I stand on the porch and watch her car until it's out of sight. As soon as I open the front door, a wall of screams hits my ears.

"Dad said you have to take your medicine!" Eliza's standing over Coco, a small cup of purple liquid in her hand.

"I don't want to." Coco is sitting on the floor. "It's gross."

"It doesn't matter if it's gross. You need to take it."

"No!" Coco gets up and runs up the stairs. "And you can't make me."

"Fine!" Eliza screams. "Get an infection! It doesn't matter to me." She pours the medicine back into the bottle and shoves the bottle into the refrigerator.

"What are you doing home?" Eliza asks. "I thought you had a date with Mom." She puts air quotes around the word "date."

"She had to go back to work," I say.

Eliza shakes her head. "She's unbelievable," she mutters under her breath. "I guess she couldn't be bothered to come in and check on Coco."

"She had to run," I say. "Something about a client."

"Right, and anyway, Coco's ice-cream date is on Mondays. Can't mess with the calendar."

"Do you have ice-cream dates with Mom?"

Eliza laughs. "Not if I can help it."

For a minute I consider telling Eliza what I was going to tell Mom, but before I can, she pulls her phone out of her pocket, puts her headphones in, and makes her way up to her room.

I sit down at the kitchen table and get started on my homework. Just as I'm halfway through my math worksheet, my phone rings. When I see Kellan's name, my stomach drops, and I immediately think something's terribly wrong. Kellan always texts.

I answer my phone. "Are you okay?"

Kellan laughs, which makes my whole body instantly relax.

"I'm better than okay," he says. "I'm going back to school!"

"What?" I almost drop the phone, but I catch it before it hits the floor. "How—what?" My brain has forgotten how to form words, probably because it's too busy swirling with conflicting feelings. I'm thrilled for Kellan. I'm worried for Kellan. And if I'm being honest, I'm worried for myself. How will Kellan fit in with my new world at school?

"Apparently, my mom's been planning this for a few weeks. She didn't want to tell me until everything was finalized. Which now it is!"

"Wow." The word comes out as more shocked than excited.

"You okay, Mols?" Kellan sounds sad, like I just popped his favorite balloon.

"Me?" I clear my throat, hoping to also clear my head. "Of course! This is great news. I'm just—I'm just surprised. After our walk today . . . I mean, you weren't feeling well—"

Kellan lowers his voice. "Yeah, I didn't tell her that part."

"Do you think you should? What if it's dangerous?"

Kellan chuckles. "It's not dangerous. And anyway, since I heard the news, I feel great. Better than ever. And that's the truth."

Kellan's enthusiasm is contagious. No matter how I feel, the important thing is that he's happy.

"This is great news, Kels. I can't wait to see you in school. When do you come back?"

"First thing next week," he says, as happy as I've ever heard him.

After we hang up, I try to focus on my homework, but the only thing I can think about is Kellan. Kellan and Robert. Kellan and Christina. Kellan and me. How will I juggle my old life with my new life? I put my head down on the kitchen table. I wish I were back in second grade. Life was so much easier then.

chapter

* 20 *

MRS. BINGHAM OFFERS TO GIVE ME A RIDE TO SCHOOL
so Kellan and I can go in together on his first day back.

Kellan's already in the back of the car when I get to
their house, and he waves at me from the window as I walk
up the driveway. He's way too excited for a day at school,
and I cringe as I wonder if Christina, Nina, Robert, and
Wade will accept him.

"Good morning!" Mrs. Bingham greets me as I slide
into the backseat next to Kellan.

"Best morning ever," Kellan says. He's wearing blue jeans
and a blue-and-white-striped polo shirt. He looks nice. Cute,
even. I'm hoping this will not go unnoticed by Christina.

"Are you sure you're ready for this?" I whisper to
Kellan.

"I'm so ready," he whispers back, a huge grin taking up half his face.

"Now, remember, Kellan," Mrs. Bingham says, glancing at him in the rearview mirror, "if you're uncomfortable, or tired, or *anything,* go to the nurse and have her call me."

Kellan rolls his eyes. "I know, Mom. We've been over this a hundred times."

"Then a hundred and one can't hurt," she says. "Molly, you'll look out for him?"

"Yes," I promise. And then wish I hadn't.

Mrs. Bingham pulls into a handicapped spot near the school's front entrance. I scoot out of the car and wait for Kellan to adjust his leg braces, which his mother is making him use.

"Want me to take your backpack?" I ask, which is still in the backseat of the car.

"No, I can take it," Kellan says. "But can you hand it to me?"

I reach into the car, grab his backpack, and give it to him. Rather than sling it onto one shoulder like I do, he secures it on both shoulders. He winces once, and I come *this close* to telling Mrs. Bingham that he looks like he's in pain. But I know that would destroy Kellan, so I keep my mouth shut.

I hold the front door open for Kellan, but I'm not

sure it makes much of a difference. Kids are pouring into the building, and Kellan has to brace himself for the onslaught. I squeeze my eyes shut as a clumsy sixth grader almost knocks him over. I breathe a big sigh of relief when he makes it to the office in one piece.

"We have to meet with the principal to go over your schedule," Mrs. Bingham tells Kellan.

"Let's do it." Kellan's whole face lights up. "Mols, I'll see you soon."

"See you soon." I return the smile, and I wonder if he can tell that it's fake.

I walk into first period and find Christina, Nina, Robert, and Wade huddled around Christina's desk. Robert waves me over.

"Hey," he says. "We're just finishing our homework."

Sure enough, they all have their worksheets out, and they're frantically writing down answers, glancing at the clock every few seconds.

"Did you finish yours?" Christina asks.

"Oh, yeah." I pull my sheet out of my backpack, and Christina grabs it out of my hands before I can even set it down on the desk.

"Thanks," she says, and copies down everything that I wrote.

Mrs. Littman is nowhere in sight, but I'm sure she'll

freak out if she sees what's happening here. And I don't think she'll give me any more free passes.

"You guys," I say in a hushed tone, "Mrs. Littman is going to be back any minute now—"

"Which is why you just have to let us concentrate on getting these answers down," Christina says, not looking up from her paper.

I open my mouth to say something else, but Robert elbows me slightly and whispers in my ear, "Just go with it. Rumor has it she's giving out invitations tomorrow."

I snap my mouth shut, and my heart does figure eights in my chest. Tomorrow? Has Christina had enough time to really get to know me? What if I don't get an invitation? Will Robert, Wade, and Nina forget about me? Will I go back to being invisible?

"Done." Christina shoves her worksheet into her backpack, and I snatch mine off of her desk. Mrs. Littman walks in two seconds later.

I dart over to my own seat and rub my sweaty palms on my jeans. That was a close one. From behind me, Robert kicks my chair, and when I turn around, he gives me a big smile and a thumbs-up. I smile back, because I just can't help myself.

"Okay, class," Mrs. Littman begins. "Please pass your

homework assignment to the front of the room."

As Mrs. Littman collects the worksheets, the classroom door opens. Kellan is standing in the doorway, backpack securely placed on his back, leaning on his braces.

"You must be Kellan." Mrs. Littman claps her hands together, like Kellan is a surprise Christmas gift that arrived on her doorstep.

"Yes, I am." Kellan smiles at her and then waves at me. "Hey, Mols."

I sink down into my chair. It's a good thing I'm sitting in front of Robert so he can't see how red my face is. Behind me somewhere, someone snickers. I don't even have to look to see who it is. I already know it's Christina.

"I believe there's an empty desk over there." Mrs. Littman points to the seat next to Nina's. I can't bring myself to turn around and watch Kellan get settled in. Instead, I stay motionless in my chair and stare straight ahead. I remain in this exact position for the next forty-five minutes.

When the bell rings, I'm paralyzed. Do I wait for Christina, Nina, Robert, and Wade, like I usually do now, or do I wait for Kellan?

"What does the rest of your day look like, Mols?" Kellan's voice rings out from behind me.

"Um, pre-algebra next, then history, then social studies." My voice is barely above a whisper. Kellan is adjusting his backpack onto his shoulders again. Christina is directly behind him as he makes his way up the aisle.

"Hey, *Mols,*" Christina says, completely mocking my nickname. "Want to walk to class together?"

"Oh, uhhh, sure." Lately, I've been walking to class with her and the group, but she's never actually asked me before. We just sort of walk. I turn to Kellan. "What about you?"

"I have social studies fourth period too!" He says this like he's just won the Boston Marathon.

"Well, come on." Christina pulls at my arm. "I don't want to be late."

"Okay," I say to Christina, then look at Kellan. "See you there?"

But Christina pulls me away before I even hear his answer.

Later that morning, when I get to social studies, Kellan is already there. He's sitting next to Dylan, who was in our fourth-grade class, and he and Kellan were sort of friendly. Relief washes over me when I see them talking. At least I don't have to be responsible for Kellan in this class.

When the bell rings, Kellan meets me at my desk.

"Looks like lunch is next." He's studying his schedule.

I nod. "Yep."

"Good." Kellan shoves the paper into his pocket. "I'm starving. And I'm totally buying all the chocolate chip cookies they have."

I smile, then look around. Everyone must have left while Kellan and I were talking. Nina, Christina, Robert—none of them even waited for me. Emptiness fills my chest. Kellan's been here only half a day and already they've forgotten about me.

Kellan, Dylan, and I head to lunch. Kellan and Dylan are talking about some video game that I've never heard of. When we reach the cafeteria, Kellan's eyes get huge.

"There's so many people," he mumbles to himself as he scans the rows and rows of tables. "Where—how do I get lunch?"

"Molly!" Nina calls to me from our usual table, patting the chair next to her. "Come join us."

If I weren't in a room filled with two hundred kids, I'd probably cry tears of joy. They didn't forget about me after all.

"The lunch line starts there," I tell Kellan, pointing to the kids waiting for their daily slop. "Cookies are next to the cashier."

"Okay." He nods, hesitantly making his way to the line. I should probably go with him. I turn back to the lunch table. Nina's waving me over.

I glance back at Kellan, who's now standing in line. He seems okay. He can probably do this without me.

I decide to join my friends at our table. Everyone says hi to me, except Christina. She just kind of nods in my general direction. I'm talking to Nina about the social studies homework when Kellan comes over, a tray balanced carefully in his hands.

Christina stares at us, and my cheeks instantly feel hot.

"You didn't save me a seat," he says.

"Oh, sorry." Now my ears are burning.

"Yeah, this table is full," Christina says.

Kellan's leaning on his braces in order to get a better grip on his tray.

"I'm really sorry," I say quietly.

Kellan scrunches up his face like he's confused. I wonder if he's waiting for me to move to another table where there's room for both of us. But I can't do that. Christina is getting ready to hand out invitations, and I can't risk upsetting her now.

Kellan looks around at the crowded cafeteria, and his face goes pale. I'm scouring my mind, looking for something to say, when Dylan calls Kellan's name from a few tables over.

"Kellan!" He waves. "Come sit here."

Kellan sees him, and relief floods his face. He turns and walks toward Dylan's table without saying a word to me.

"Looks like that kid found his people," Christina says with a smirk.

"What?" I'm not sure what she means by that.

"You know." Christina juts her chin out. "He's at the nerd table. It's a good place for him. He'll be happy there."

Robert and Wade laugh. I try to smile so Christina thinks I'm not upset by what she said, but I feel like I've been punched in the gut. I glance back at Kellan, who's unwrapping a burrito on his tray. Dylan is talking to him, so I feel better that he's not alone.

And even though it hurts to hear, maybe Christina's right. Maybe Kellan has found his people, and maybe I have too.

It's just that I thought Kellan and I would be friends forever.

When school ends, Kellan and I wait out front for his mom to pick us up. Kellan's unusually quiet, but it's not the comfortable kind of quiet that is easy between us. This time the silence feels like a sonic boom.

"So." I try to keep the conversation light. "How was your first day?"

"It was fine," Kellan says.

"See, I told you school isn't as exciting as you remember." I give him a friendly nudge, but he doesn't react.

"It's just . . ." Kellan takes a deep breath. "You seem really different lately."

My whole body tenses up, and I feel like I'm wearing a suit of armor. "What do you mean?"

"I mean—" Kellan sighs. "It's like we're not even best friends in school. You act like you don't know me at all."

My heart speeds up inside my chest, and I can hear it thumping all the way up to my ears. "Well, what am I supposed to do? I have friends at school now. I can't drop them all of a sudden because you're here."

"I never said you should drop your new friends." Kellan looks at me, then down at the ground. "But I don't get what you see in them."

"They're fun. And they like me."

"They like you?" Kellan snorts. "They don't even know you."

"Of course they know me!" My voice sounds squeaky when it comes out of my mouth.

"Oh, yeah?" Kellan's leaning on his leg braces now,

like he doesn't have the strength to hold himself up. "Do they know that you still sleep with the teddy bear you got when you were seven months old? Do they know that you've eaten the exact same thing for breakfast every day for the past ten years? Do they know that you can't fall asleep without a night-light? And do they know that your parents are fighting and might get—"

"Okay, I get it!" I yell. Tears are pricking my eyes, but I blink them away. "They might not know everything about me, but that comes with time, Kellan."

"They'll never learn about you if you constantly pretend to be someone else."

"I'm not pretending." I clench my jaw. "Maybe you don't know everything about me either."

"I thought I did," Kellan says, and his voice trembles a little.

"Well, I hope you didn't want to come to school only because of me." I put my hands on my hips. "That's a lot of pressure, you know."

Kellan snaps his head up. "Seriously, Molly?" The fact that he used my real name is a bad sign. "Is that what you're worried about?"

My stomach is swirling, and I feel like I might throw up. "I don't know. Maybe."

"Don't sweat it," Kellan says just as his mom's car

approaches us. "Consider yourself off the hook."

"Kellan, I—" But he puts his hand up to stop me. Mrs. Bingham's car pulls up to the curb, and he's all smiles as he climbs in—to the front seat.

"How was your first day?" Mrs. Bingham gives Kellan a kiss on the cheek.

"It was great." Kellan's fake smile lights up the car.

"I'm so happy to hear that!" Mrs. Bingham pulls away from the curb and out of the school parking lot. "It must have been great to be together again, huh, Molly?"

"Yep." I follow Kellan's lead and muster pretend enthusiasm. "It was."

"I'm so glad all went well! How about we go get smoothies to celebrate?"

"Awww, Mom," Kellan says. "We'd totally love to, but we have a ton of homework."

I stare at the back of his head. We actually didn't get a lot of homework today, and the one math worksheet that I know about will probably take Kellan all of ten minutes to finish.

"Well, schoolwork does come first, I suppose. We'll do it another time." Mrs. Bingham pulls into my driveway.

"Thanks so much for the ride," I say.

"See you tomorrow," Kellan says, as if we are still the best of friends who had the best of days.

And it's then that I realize how much of the truth Kellan's been keeping from his mom. He doesn't share his pain, his fear, or any thought that might seem even a little bit sad.

He reserved all of that for me. And if I'm not his friend anymore, who will he share that with?

I open the front door to my house, run upstairs to my bedroom, and cry.

chapter
* 21 *

AFTER A GOOD HOUR OF SOBBING I ATTEMPT TO DO
my math homework. I get one problem solved before my
phone beeps.

A text from Robert.

Christina's made her decision. Invitations going out tmro!

My heartbeat speeds up, and I type back a quick
response.

Any idea who made the list?

I bite my lower lip while I wait for Robert's reply.

Always a surprise. C likes to keep people waiting.

I close my math workbook. There's no way I can concentrate on homework now. If I'm on that list, my whole
life will change. I'll officially be part of the group, and that
means I won't have to always be on edge with Christina.

I can just be myself instead of having to work so hard to be her friend. And once I'm in, I can get Kellan in too. Then he'll forgive me for acting weird and we'll all be friends.

It's the perfect plan.

All I need is an invitation to the Birthday Bash.

I give up on math and head downstairs for a snack. I'm just toasting some bread for a PB&J when Coco plows through the front door, chocolate smeared all over her face. My mom follows her in, talking on her cell phone.

"I don't care what he says," Mom is saying. "Those are billable hours. Look, we'll talk about this when I get back to the office." She throws the cell phone into her purse.

"Mommy and me had ice cream!" Coco is twirling around the kitchen.

"Coco, watch your cast," Mom says, and then turns to me. "Hi there, Molly."

"Hi, Mom." I spread some peanut butter on my toast.

"How are you?" She puts her purse on the kitchen counter.

"Fine," I say. "You?"

"Just busy." Mom looks around the kitchen. "Where's Eliza?"

I shrug. "No idea."

Mom sighs, loudly. "She should be home doing her

homework. This is a crucial year for her. Her grades aren't good. She needs to be worrying about college, and instead, she's out doing who-knows-what."

Mom pulls her cell phone out of her purse. She's holding the phone with one hand, the other hand on her hip. After a few seconds she starts talking. "Eliza. It's almost five o'clock. Where are you? You need to be home doing your homework. Call me back."

"She doesn't listen to her voice mail," I say, taking a bite of my sandwich.

"What?" Mom's voice is sharp, like she's mad at me for being the messenger.

"You have to text her," I say.

"I don't have time for this," Mom says. "I have to get back to the office. When she finally comes home, tell her to call me."

Mom kisses me on the cheek. "I'll see you soon, Molly."

Maybe it's the anxiety of not knowing if I'll be invited to Christina's Birthday Bash or maybe it's the stress I feel over the fight Kellan and I had, but I want my mom to stay. It's not that we're even close or that I miss her since she's not been living at home. I don't know what it is, but I do know that just having her home makes me feel a tiny bit better.

"How's Coco's arm? Healing okay?" I blurt it out, just as my mom heads out of the kitchen.

"Yes, yes." She waves her hand in front of her. "It's healing fine."

"When will the cast be off?" I follow her to the front door.

"A few weeks." She puts one hand on the doorknob, then turns back to look at me. "Why the sudden interest in your sister's arm?"

I shrug and start twirling my hair. "Just curious."

"We'll know more at her doctor's appointment next week," Mom says. "I'll be sure to keep you posted."

From the other side of the door, a loud blast of heavy-metal music plays. Mom purses her lips and peeks out the window.

"Oh, for crying out loud." She opens the front door and steps out onto the front porch. "Eliza! Get inside right now."

Over her shoulder I can see Eliza in the driveway with a bunch of her friends. The car radio is blaring. At the sight of my mom her friends pile in the car and pull away. Eliza is standing in the driveway, mouth hanging open.

"What is wrong with you?" Eliza's hands are placed firmly on her hips.

"I should ask you the same question." Mom's heels

make clomp-clomp-clomping noises as she goes down the porch steps and comes face-to-face with Eliza.

"I got a ride home from school," Eliza says. "What's the big deal?"

"The big deal is . . ." Mom looks at her watch. "It's almost five o'clock, and I'm sure you have homework to do."

Eliza crosses her arms. "Are you serious?"

"Of course I'm serious," Mom says. "I've seen your grades, Eliza. You'll never get into a good college unless you buckle down. Your entire future is at stake, and you're wasting it on some derelicts!"

"Derelicts?" Eliza's voice is so high-pitched, I hardly recognize it. "Those people are my friends. They're good to me. Which is more than I can say for you."

Mom flinches, as if Eliza slapped her. "And what is that supposed to mean?"

"You show up once a week and lecture me. What kind of parenting is that? You lost your right to tell me what to do when you moved out." Eliza pushes past Mom, and it's only then that I realize I'm standing in the doorway. I slink inside to get out of her way. She runs past me and marches up the steps to her room. Her door slams, and a few seconds later the music blares.

By the time I step out onto the front porch, Mom is already in her car, backing out of the driveway.

Eliza is locked in her room, Coco is parked in front of the television, and Dad won't be home from work for at least another hour. The only thing I want to do is ride my bike to Kellan's. But I can't, because he's not talking to me.

I flop down onto the porch swing and rock myself back and forth until Dad comes home with pizza.

chapter

22

I TEXT KELLAN THE NEXT MORNING AND TELL HIM MY dad will drive me to school. I ask him if he wants a ride. He doesn't text back.

The hallway is buzzing. There are a flock of kids gathered around Christina, who's laughing and flipping her hair and generally looking like the queen of the world.

Did she already give out the invitations? Are the people surrounding her the ones who made the cut? And does that mean I didn't?

"Hey," Robert pats me on the back. "What's up? You look like you're gonna hurl."

"I do?" I try to smile, but my stomach is in knots, wondering if I made the Birthday Bash list.

"Yeah. You okay?"

"Just wondering what's going on over there." I point to Christina's locker. "Did she already hand out the invitations?"

"Not yet," Robert says. "She likes to milk this."

"Is that why all those people are hovering around her?"

"Yep," Robert says. "They all want an invite to the biggest party of the year."

"Why aren't you over there?" I ask.

Robert smiles. "I've been invited for the last four years. I'm pretty sure I'm a shoo-in."

"Must be nice," I say.

"Don't worry." Robert puts his arm around me, and little goose bumps pop up on my skin. "I put in a good word for you."

"Really? Think I'll make the cut?"

Robert shrugs. "I hope so."

I can't help but smile, even though part of me wonders if he'll still like me if I don't make the birthday list.

Kellan hardly talks to me all morning. At lunch he sits with Dylan again.

Christina barely talks to me all morning too, and although I sit at our usual table for lunch, she's surrounded by so many other people that I doubt she even notices I'm there. I get up to buy two chocolate chip cookies—both for me, since I doubt Kellan would accept one even if I offered it to him. I'm just paying for the cookies when I bump into Nina, who's pulling a bunch of napkins out of the napkin holder.

"Hey, Molly," Nina says. "Taylor spilled a bottle of juice right in front of Christina."

"Oh no," I say. "That's bad timing."

Nina gives a halfhearted smile. "Yeah, I thought Taylor was going to start to cry. Luckily, it missed Christina and mostly spilled in Wade's lap."

I giggle at that. "People go kind of crazy about this party, huh?"

Nina nods, then opens her mouth like she's about to say something, but then she closes it again.

"I guess I'd better get these napkins over to Christina," she says. "See you over there."

Kellan and Dylan are sitting at a nearby table. He doesn't make any sign that he notices me here. Then again, I don't make any sign that I notice him, either. I take one of the cookies out of the package and eat it. I gently place the other one in the front pocket of my sweater.

The next few classes pass by like normal, but things feel incomplete. Sure, I hang out a little with Nina and Robert in the hallway between periods, but something inside of me feels empty.

On my way to my last class, I see Kellan at his locker, piling books into his backpack. He's alone; no Dylan in sight. A lump grows in the back of my throat as I watch him. Even though I'm standing five feet away from him, it feels like he's on the other side of the world.

He catches me watching him, and I'm shocked when he gives me a little wave. Without checking with the rest of me, my legs take this as an opening. They speed-walk to his locker.

"I saved this for you." I pull the cookie out of my pocket.

"Sweet!" He takes it from my hand. "Thanks."

And then we both start talking at the same time.

"No, let me go first." I take a deep breath. "I'm sorry. I haven't been a very good best friend. I ruined your first day back at school. I'm sorry."

Kellan shakes his head. "It's my fault. I got jealous of your new friends and just felt left out. I was acting like a baby."

"No, no," I say. "I've been the one acting like—"

"Okay, okay." Kellan puts his hand up. "How about if we say it's both of our faults and leave it at that?"

I smile. "Sounds good to me."

"Hey," Kellan says, "want to go for a practice walk after school?"

Mom already texted last night to ask if we could move

our ice-cream date to tomorrow, so that means I'm free to hang out with Kellan. I lean in and give him a little hug. "That would be awesome."

Kellan's cheeks turn pink. "Cool. Meet me outside after school. My mom can take us straight to my house."

I practically float down the hall after that. I'm so relieved that Kellan's talking to me again that for a few minutes I actually don't think about the Birthday Bash invitations.

Until Robert comes sprinting up just as I'm about to walk into Spanish class.

"Did you get one?" He's waving a glossy bright red envelope in my face.

The invitation.

"I—I don't know," I stammer. "Where would I look?"

"It would be in your locker," he says. "Quick! Let's go! Before the final warning bell rings."

Robert and I race to my locker. When I get there, I'm so nervous that I forget my locker combination.

"What are you waiting for?" Robert is bouncing on his toes.

I take a deep breath and exhale slowly. The numbers pop into my mind. I wipe my sweaty hands on my jeans and turn the knob: 34-12-24. My locker pops open, and I scan the inside for something red.

But there's nothing.

I pick up each textbook and place them all on the floor next to me. As I do, Robert picks them up and flips through the pages, in case the invitation got caught inside one of them. After all my books and folders are out of my locker and scattered all around us, I finally turn around and look at him.

"I'm really sorry," he says. "I thought for sure—"

I hold up my hand. If he keeps talking, I'm going to burst into tears, and that's the last thing I need to do right now. I pick everything up and pile it back into my locker. I have no idea if Robert is still behind me. I'm afraid to look. The second bell rings, which means we have one minute to get to class. I close my locker and turn around. Robert is gone.

The tears leak one by one out of my eyes, and I wipe them with the back of my hand. I thought all these years of being a nobody were over. I will never be important. Never.

The hallway is almost empty now. I shake my head, square my shoulders, and head back toward my next class. Less than one hour until I can cry my eyes out. But for now, I have to keep it together.

I'm almost at my Spanish classroom when I hear Robert call my name. I turn around to see him running my way.

"Molly!" Robert stops in front of me, out of breath. "She's not finished yet."

"What?" I ask him, clutching my textbook to my chest.

"Christina isn't finished handing out the invitations yet."

My stomach flip-flops. "Do you know if I'm getting one?"

"No. It's top secret. She won't say anything until all of them are out."

"Then how do you know she's not finished?"

"I ran into her after I left your locker. I saw her slide an invitation into Wade's locker, and she still had a couple more envelopes in her hand. Then the bell rang, and she told me she'd have to finish after this period."

"So there's still a chance?" I suck in my breath, afraid to start breathing again. I just want this whole waiting time to be over.

"I'd say there's a good chance." Robert smiles. "Just hang in there for a little while longer."

And then he runs off. I take my seat in Spanish and watch the clock for the next forty-five minutes. When the final bell finally rings, I slowly gather up my things. I want to be sure Christina has enough time to put the invitation in my locker.

The hallway is buzzing. The kids with red envelopes flash them to anyone who walks by, and the kids who don't have them are whispering and pointing to those who do.

I keep my eyes straight ahead of me as I head to my locker.

chapter
* 23 *

BY THE TIME I REACH MY LOCKER, MY HEART IS beating so fast, I'm afraid I might pass out. I slowly turn the lock, and when my locker pops open, I see it immediately.

A bright red envelope, resting on top of my pile of books.

My body feels like it's a balloon that's been released into the sky. My name, written in sparkly silver calligraphy, stares up at me, and this time the tears that well up behind my eyes are happy ones.

"You got it!" Robert's voice booms behind me.

I grab the red envelope and hold it up. "I got it."

"Sweet!" Robert holds his hand up for a high five, and I happily give him one.

Kids stare as they walk by, their mouths hanging open.

They elbow each other and glance at Robert and me. I'm clutching my invitation like it's an Olympic gold medal.

"Oh, wow." Alissa Steinman, a girl in our grade who I've never spoken to before, is standing behind us. "Did you get an invitation to Christina Golden's Birthday Bash Brunch?"

"She sure did." Robert's beaming with pride.

Alissa looks me up and down. "Cool. Congrats."

"Thanks," I say.

This happens a few more times with other kids I recognize but don't actually know. It's as if they see me for the first time ever. As we all pack up for the day and head toward the exits, practically every seventh grader I pass says hi to me or gives me some kind of compliment. Others just smile and wave after a quick glance at the invite.

When I meet Kellan outside, I'm still holding the red envelope in my hand.

"What's that?" he asks.

"Oh," I answer casually. "It's an invitation to Christina's Birthday Bash."

"Christina's what?"

Kellan's probably the only one in the whole middle school who doesn't know about her birthday party. "It's this big party Christina throws every year for her birthday. Maybe I can get you an invitation?"

The words pour out of my mouth as if they were spoken by an invisible alien living inside my body. What was I thinking?! I barely got myself an invitation. There's no way I can get Kellan one.

"Nah." He laughs. "It's okay. Thanks, though."

I let out my breath and smile. I don't know what I would have done if he actually wanted to go.

Mrs. Bingham takes us back to Kellan's, where she has watermelon waiting for us. We eat it outside in the backyard and have a contest to see who can spit the seeds the farthest. My seeds practically dribble out of my mouth and land just in front of my feet. As always, Kellan wins the spitting contest.

He does really well on our walk, too. We don't even stop at our usual bench. He spends the first fifteen minutes talking about school—he thinks Mrs. Littman is a good teacher, he doesn't understand a word in Spanish class, and he's bummed that he can't participate in PE—and when he finally stops, I fill him in on the drama at home.

"Whoa," Kellan says. "Eliza actually said that to your mom?"

"Yep," I say.

"Whoa," Kellan says again.

"She isn't wrong, though."

Kellan nods.

"I mean," I continue, "my mom isn't around much. If she were really worried about Eliza, don't you think she'd move back home? Maybe spend more time with her?"

"I guess," Kellan says. "But isn't she in a fight with your dad?"

"They're grown-ups," I say. "They should just work it out."

"Yeah," Kellan says. "Like we did."

"Exactly." I point my finger in the air. "We made mistakes. We apologized. We got over it."

"We're so much more reasonable than grown-ups." Kellan laughs, and I do too.

"So what happens at Christina's Birthday Bash that makes it such a big deal?" Kellan asks, stopping to take a sip from the water bottle that's shoved in his pocket.

"It's a fancy brunch at her country club. We get all dressed up and eat caviar."

"Ewww, gross!" Kellan spits out his water. "Caviar is fish eggs."

I wrinkle my nose. "Well, there are also a bunch of chocolate fountains."

"I guess that's cool."

"We get picked up in a limo. There's a professional photographer and a dress-up photo booth. And I've heard the gift bags are amazing."

"Nice," Kellan says. "When is it?"

I shrug. "I'm not sure. I haven't actually opened the invitation yet."

"Well, I hope you have fun. You'll have to tell me all about it. Except for the caviar. I don't want to hear about that."

"So you're okay with the fact that I'm going to the party?" We're about a block away from Kellan's house now.

"Yeah," he says. "It's not that I don't want you to have other friends, Mols. And no offense, but I think Christina is a jerk."

"She's okay once you get to know her," I say, even though I'm not sure I believe it.

"If you say so," Kellan says. "I just want to be sure we're always friends."

"Of course," I say. "Best friends."

After more watermelon and another seed-spitting contest (I lose again), Mrs. Bingham drives me home. Eliza and Coco are playing video games when I walk in. I haven't talked to Eliza since her fight with Mom. I consider asking her how she's doing, but I'm not sure I'm ready to hear the answer.

Instead, I go up to my room and get ready for homework. I pull the invitation out of my backpack and flip it around in my hands. I place my finger under the seal and gently pull so that the envelope opens up. I pull the invitation out. It's made of a shiny black paper with red trim.

You are cordially invited to

Christina's Birthday Bash Brunch

The Club at Fairview

Saturday, May 20

10:00 a.m.–1:00 p.m.

Semiformal attire

I hug the invitation to my chest. This party will change my life. And I know, once Christina gets to know me better, she'll welcome Kellan into her circle too.

I pull a red marker out of my desk drawer so I can write the date on my wall calendar. As my hand finds May 20, I freeze.

Oh no. No, no, no.

May 20 is already circled.

It's the date of the Muscular Dystrophy Walk with Kellan.

chapter

24

I FEEL LIKE I JUST ATE A LOAF OF MOLDY BREAD. MY stomach is swooping and swirling, but I know what I have to do.

Of course I have to go to the walk. It's Kellan, and it's the most important day of the year for him.

But then again, my entire reputation rides on this party. If I back out, Christina will never speak to me again and I'll go back to being an outcast. And Robert. What would Robert think if I bailed on the party?

I'm sure I'll figure something out.

I think I'll figure something out.

I hope I'll figure something out.

Just because I'm curious, I google "semiformal" and find out that it means fancy, but not ball-gown fancy. If

I do go to the party, I'll need something to wear. I open my closet door and scan the contents. Nothing in there says "semiformal." I consider calling Mom and asking her to take me dress shopping, but the thought of spending hours at the mall with her makes me feel like I just swallowed a bowling ball. And she'd probably make me get a dress that she likes instead of one I like.

There's only one person who can help me. The question is . . . will she?

I take a few steps across the hall to Eliza's room. The door is closed, but music is playing, softer than it usually is. I knock twice.

"What?" her voice calls from the other side of the door.

"Ummm. It's Molly."

"What do you want?"

I take a step closer to the door, as if this will somehow help her to understand that I come in peace.

"I need help."

Silence.

"With a dress."

The door opens, and I'm standing so close to it that I practically fall into her room.

"Why don't you ask Mom?" She stares at me.

I blink. "Because I thought I'd ask you."

Eliza stares at me for a second longer. She's wearing jeans and a hoodie. There's nothing special about her clothes, but she knows how to accessorize to make them look unique. A bangle of bracelets hangs from her wrist, and her hair is tied up in a messy bun. Her earrings are the exact same color as her sandals, and her fingernail polish matches the tint on her toes.

"What's the dress for?" Eliza steps inside her bedroom, and I follow.

"It's for a party that I might go to." I twirl a purple strand of hair around my finger.

"A party you might go to?" Eliza opens her closet door. "That's not very helpful. I mean, what kind of party is it?"

"Christina's Birthday Bash Brunch."

Eliza raises her eyebrows. "I have no idea what that is."

Right. I keep thinking everybody knows what that is. "It's a semiformal brunch at Christina's parents' country club."

"Which club?" Eliza scans her closet.

"Fairview."

Eliza whistles. "Wow. Fancy schmancy."

"Yeah," I say. "We're taking a limo."

"What kind of seventh-grade party is this?" Eliza shakes her head.

"A big one," I say. "Which is why I need help finding a dress."

"You've come to the right place," Eliza says. "Let's see what I have here."

Eliza crawls deep into her closet and pulls out a few bins stored in the back—bins I hadn't even seen before. I think they multiply in Eliza's closet while she sleeps.

She opens the lid of one of them and rummages around until she finds what she's looking for. "Aha!"

I kneel down on the floor next to her. She holds up a black taffeta dress with spaghetti straps.

"Stand up," she demands. "Let's see if this might work."

I do as she says, and she holds the dress in front of me. "Go try it on." She hands me the dress, and I scamper off into my room with it. I slip it on as fast as I can, since I know how quickly Eliza's moods can change. In five minutes she may decide she doesn't want to help me anymore.

I race back into her room, and she takes a few steps back, eyeing me up and down.

"Add this." She hurls a silver shrug sweater at me, and I throw it on.

Eliza stares at me for a few seconds and then nods. She rummages around in her closet some more until she finds a pair of silver sandals with a heel higher than I've ever worn before.

"Put these on."

I sit down on her bed and tighten the straps. I stand up, wobbly at first, and Eliza claps her hands together. "Perfect! You just need some jewelry to top it off. I'll find something for you."

"You think I look okay?" I look down at myself, but it's hard to get the whole picture.

"See for yourself." She points to the full-length mirror behind her closet door.

I stumble across her carpet and make a note to myself to practice walking in heels. When I reach the mirror, I actually gasp.

I look like a completely different person. A fancy person. A person who eats caviar and rides in limos and gets invited to semiformal parties.

"Wow," I say.

"You look good," Eliza says.

I turn to face her. "Thank you so much."

"No problem. I'll do your makeup for the party if you want. If you decide to go."

"Yeah," I say. If I decide to go. "That would be great."

"Now get out." Eliza points to the door. "I'm busy."

I reach the door before I turn around. "Thanks, Eliza."

She nods, and I close the door behind me. I'm changing

into my regular clothes when my phone buzzes. It's a text from Mom, and it's to Dad, Eliza, and me.

Family meeting 5 pm Friday.

I lay back on my bed and groan.

Family meetings are *never* good.

chapter
* 25 *

"ONLY EIGHT DAYS UNTIL THE BIRTHDAY BASH," ROBERT says as we're walking to social studies Friday at school.

My stomach flip-flops. The party and the walk are next weekend, and I still haven't made up my mind. Everything's been so peaceful that I'm afraid to ruin it. I spend lunch with the crew at Christina's table, and Kellan spends it with Dylan and his friends. Kellan and I sometimes talk in the halls, and we spend every day after school together. It's the best of both worlds.

"Do you know what you're wearing?" Robert asks.

"What?" I look down at my clothes.

"To the party." He nudges me gently in the side.

"Oh, yeah—I, uhhh . . . uhhh," I stammer. "My sister helped me pick out a dress."

"Hi, Robert! Hi, Molly!" Alissa Steinman and Taylor O'Neil wave at us from across the hall. This happens so often now that it's hard to finish a conversation. I wonder if this is how celebrities feel when they try to go out in public.

"What color is it?" Robert asks.

"What color is what?"

"Your dress," Robert says. I really don't want to talk about this.

"Oh." My cheeks and ears feel instantly hot. "Black. With silver accessories."

"Cool," Robert says. "I'll match you."

I stop walking when we reach social studies. "You'll wear a black dress with silver accessories?"

"Ha-ha." Robert smiles. "I'll wear a black suit with a silver tie. So we can match. You know, like people do at proms and stuff."

The back of my neck starts to tingle. Don't boyfriends and girlfriends match? Does this means he wants to be my boyfriend?

"That would be cool," I say, and I rub away the little beads of sweat that pop up on my forehead. I picture Robert and I holding hands while we walk down the hallways together, and even though it's only in my imagination, my entire face gets hot.

At lunch Christina tells us about the menu for the

Birthday Bash. There will be cinnamon-stuffed French toast, four-berry pancakes, eggs Benedict, breakfast burritos, vegetable frittata, quiche, apple pie waffles, chocolate-banana smoothies, and an entire dessert table. And even though I already finished lunch, my mouth waters just thinking about it.

Just as I'm cleaning up the table, Kellan walks over with Dylan.

"Coming over after school today?" Kellan says.

"Sure." I nod.

Once Kellan leaves, Christina steps closer to me. "You're still friends with him?"

I shrug. "Yeah. I've known him forever."

"I guess," Christina says. "But don't you think you've outgrown him?"

"I don't know," I say quietly, crumpling my paper lunch bag into a ball.

"You're friends with us now." Christina points to herself and Nina, who's staring down at the floor. "You don't need anyone else."

My mind freezes, and I can't think of a response to this. Is she threatening me, letting me know in her Christina way that I can't be friends with Kellan?

"Gotta go to class." Christina gives me a smirk. "You coming?"

Christina, Nina, and I walk to class together, but no one says a word.

One thing is clear, though.

I've made up my mind.

Kellan and I are taking a practice walk after school when he starts talking about the Muscular Dystrophy Walk. "I can't believe it's only a week away."

Now's my chance.

I'll just tell Kellan I can't go to the walk. He'll be okay with it. He even said that he's fine with me having new friends. Plus, we've been having some great practice walks lately, and he really seems to be feeling better. I'm sure he'll understand much better than Robert or Christina would.

"You'll do great. You're ready." I take a deep breath to psych myself up.

"Yeah," he says. "But I'm still nervous."

"You're going to have a good time."

"*We're* going to have a good time," he says, and I stop walking. Suddenly, I can't catch my breath.

"You okay, Mols?" he asks.

I nod. "Just need a minute." My heart is beating so fast, I'm afraid it's going to explode. I close my eyes and take another deep breath, hoping to calm myself down.

"What's wrong?" Kellan's voice is shaky.

"Nothing. It's just—" I open my eyes. There's that crease in Kellan's forehead. He's worried about me, which makes me feel even yuckier than I already do. "I have to tell you something."

"Okay," Kellan says. "Why don't we go sit down?"

Luckily, we're only a few feet away from our favorite bench. I shuffle over to it, Kellan holding on to my arm, and we both sit down.

"What is it, Mols?" Kellan bites his lip.

"The walk is at the same time as Christina's Birthday Bash." The words fly out of my mouth and cling to the air between us.

Kellan's mouth forms an O shape. "I'm really sorry, Mols. Is Christina mad at you?"

"What?" I blink a few times, not sure why he thinks Christina would be mad at me.

"For not going to her party. Is she mad?"

"I—I don't think—" I try to speak, but there's a sob threatening to erupt out of my throat. I swallow it down. "I am going to her party."

Kellan's mouth falls open. "But how can you go to her party and also go to the walk with me?"

"I can't." I stare down at my hands.

"So . . ." Kellan stands up. "Are you telling me you're

not coming with me to the walk because you're going to Christina's party instead?"

I stand up too. "Yes, but—"

"I was counting on you." Kellan is shaking his head slowly, as if he's trying to get my words situated inside his brain. "What if I need you? What if I can't do it by myself?"

"You can, Kellan!"

"You don't know that. You told me you'd be there. You said you'd push me in the wheelchair if I needed you to." Kellan's face is now bright red.

"But you won't need me to! You can—"

"You said you'd be there for me." Kellan's voice is quieter now.

"I'm sorry," I whisper. "It's just that I think this will be good for both of us."

Kellan squints his eyes. "Good for both of us?"

"Yes." I reach for his hand. "See, if I'm in with Christina and all those guys, then soon they'll get to know you, and then you'll be in with them too."

"Why would I want to be in with them?" Kellan pulls his hand away from mine.

Why wouldn't he want to be in with them? "Because everybody knows them. And everybody wants to be friends with them."

"I don't want to be friends with them," Kellan says.

"Why not?" I bite the inside of my lip.

"Why would I?" Kellan throws his hands in the air. "They've never been nice to me, and in fact, Christina's actually been mean to me. They don't have any of the same interests that I have. Just because they're popular doesn't make them good people."

"So you don't even want to try to get to know them?" My pulse booms inside my ears.

"What does this have to do with me, anyway?" Kellan asks. "You're the one who was invited to the party, I wasn't."

"Right! And if I go this year, maybe I can get you invited next year—"

Kellan interrupts me. "I don't care about some stupid party. I care about this walk. And I thought you did too."

"I do." I step closer to him, but he takes a step backward. "But I can't be in two places at once."

"So you've made your decision, then?" Kellan asks.

"Yes," I say quietly. "Are you mad?"

Kellan chuckles under his breath. "Am I mad? Are you kidding?"

"Don't be mad," I say.

"You can't tell me how to feel." Kellan turns around. "I'm going home."

"I'll walk with you," I say.

"Don't bother. I can do it myself. You just said so."

I watch him go, unsteady on his feet. As soon as he's out of sight, the sob that's been lingering in my throat lets loose. I don't know how long I cry, but after there aren't any tears left, I start the long walk back to my house.

Alone.

chapter
26

MY MOM'S CAR IS IN THE DRIVEWAY WHEN I GET HOME.
And then I remember.

Family meeting.

Family meetings aren't a regular thing in our house.
We've had only a few of them, but they're quite memorable.
Mom calls family meetings only when something has gone
very, very wrong.

Mom and Dad are already seated at the kitchen table
when I walk in. Mom's holding a paper coffee cup, and
Dad is leaning back in his chair with his eyes closed.

"Where's your sister?" Mom asks.

"Which one?"

"Which one do you think?" Mom glares at me, as if it's
my fault Eliza's not here.

I glance at the clock on the microwave. "You said five o'clock. She still has three minutes."

Mom takes a long, loud slurp of her coffee. "You might as well sit down until she gets here," she says.

I slide into my chair and wait.

Eliza comes in two minutes later. She actually laughs when she sees us all sitting there. "You guys don't waste any time," she says.

"Sit down," Mom demands.

Eliza goes to the fridge and grabs a bottle of iced tea. "Where's Coco?"

"She's upstairs watching a movie," Mom says.

"I thought this was a family meeting." Eliza opens the iced tea and takes a sip.

"Coco's not old enough to understand," Mom says, her jaw clenching.

"That's ridiculous," Eliza says. "You guys treat her like she's the family pet. How's she ever going to learn responsibility?"

"Excuse me"—Mom pushes on her chair and stands up—"but you don't get to decide how Coco is raised."

"How she's raised?" Eliza is yelling now. "The only thing raising Coco is the television and Chips Ahoy!"

"Eliza, that's enough," Dad says. But his voice sounds tired.

"You two are too busy with your own drama to raise anyone. It's too late for me, but maybe you could step up and get it right with Molly or Coco."

"You have no right to talk to us that way," Mom says. "We are excellent parents. We provide you a house to live in, food to eat, clothes to wear. Do you think you're entitled to all of that?"

"I've had a job since I was fourteen. When was the last time you bought me clothes, Mom?"

Mom opens her mouth to say something, then shuts it again.

"And yes, you do provide a house and food. But isn't that what parents are supposed to do? It's like you guys do the bare minimum on the parenting checklist and expect to be rewarded mightily."

"I can't believe how ungrateful you are," Mom says. "Maybe you should live on your own for a while and see how you like it."

Eliza laughs. "I've been living on my own for years. You want to kick me out of the house? Fine."

"Okay, okay." Dad's voice is a little louder now. "This isn't very productive."

Eliza flops down on a chair and stares at him. "What did you hope to accomplish, then?"

"We need to set some ground rules for you, Eliza. You

need a curfew, and you need to maintain a certain GPA, and you need to—"

"And what do you need to do?" Eliza interrupts him.

"This isn't about us," Mom says.

"Maybe it should be." The words come out of my mouth before I can stop them, and Mom, Dad, and Eliza stare at me as if I've sprouted a second head.

"What did you say, Molly?" Mom's using her lawyer voice, and I swallow hard.

"Well . . ." I sit up straighter in my chair, trying to make room in my stomach for the butterflies that have just hatched in it. "This is a family meeting, right? So it should be about the family, about all of us. Not just Eliza. But you guys, me, and even Coco."

"So you two are ganging up on us now? Is that what this is about?" Mom's lawyer voice is gone, and it's been replaced with a shaky, weaker version of Mom's regular voice.

"No, Mom." I take a deep breath. "Maybe Eliza makes mistakes. I know I make mistakes. But you guys make mistakes too."

Dad leans forward in his chair, his hands clasped on the table in front of him. "What kind of mistakes do you think we make, Molly?"

"You're—you're just—" I stammer to get the words

out. It's not easy to tell your parents the truth sometimes, especially when the truth will hurt their feelings. "You're not around much. You don't know what's going on in our lives. You just seem way more concerned with yourselves."

Mom doesn't say anything, but her face is hard, like she's turned into a statue.

Dad puts the palms of his hands over his eyes. "You know this hasn't been the easiest time for us," he says. "We've been having problems of our own."

"I know," I say. "But plenty of parents who are breaking up still know what's going on with their kids."

"Well, this is ridiculous." Mom stands up again, grabbing her purse off the back of her chair. "Clearly, Eliza and Molly have banded together. This is typical of this age. Maybe you two will come to your senses when you're adults and see how good you've had it."

"Oh, come on, Karen," Dad says. "Don't get like that. Stay and let's have this meeting."

"I'm not going to sit here and be ridiculed," Mom says.

"Nobody's ridiculing anyone," Dad says. "But this does need to be hashed out. It sounds like it's long overdue."

"Fine." Mom starts walking toward the door. "You all hash this out and call me when you're done. I have important things to do."

And then she's gone.

Dad, Eliza, and I sit at the table in silence. I pick at a hangnail, waiting for someone else to say something.

"Eliza," Dad finally says, "why don't you get Coco so we can finish this meeting?"

Eliza runs up the stairs and comes down with Coco trailing her.

"I want to go back to my movie. It was just getting to the good part," Coco whines.

"You can finish it later." Dad points to a chair. "Please sit down. We're having a family meeting."

"What's that?" Coco scrunches up her nose.

"It's a meeting where we all talk about what's happening in our lives, including things that might be bothering us," Dad says.

"I'm bothered that I had to stop my movie." Coco's legs are swinging from the chair.

"Well, we should talk about that," Dad says. "I think maybe you're spending too much time watching TV. What do you think?"

"I like TV," Coco says.

"I know you do," Dad says. "And I'm not saying you can't watch it anymore. But aren't there other things you like to do too?"

Coco puts her finger on her chin and thinks. "I like to paint. We do that in school sometimes."

"Wonderful!" Dad claps his hands together. "What about if we sign you up for a painting class? Would you like that?"

"Yeah," Coco says.

"And what about you, Molly?" Dad turns to me. "Is there anything you want to talk about?"

I consider spilling my guts right there, telling them all about my fight with Kellan, and my decision to go to the Birthday Bash instead of the MD Walk, and how I'm mad at Mom for walking out. But as I look at Dad's anxious face, it's too much at once. Dad's trying, and I have a feeling his parenting path will be filled with baby steps.

"Not really," I say. "Except that I think we should have family meetings more often."

"It's a date," Dad says, a huge smile covering his face.

Eliza gives me a thumbs-up under the table, and I know she's thinking what I'm thinking.

It's a good start.

chapter

* 27 *

THE NEXT WEEK AT SCHOOL IS WEIRD. THERE'S SO much excitement about the Birthday Bash. The few people who were invited can talk about nothing else, and those who weren't invited make us promise to post pictures and share details. We're all chatting about what we're wearing, who's going to sit where, and how bad we feel for everyone who's not going. Kids are constantly waving at me or seeking my advice on everything from hairstyles to history homework. I am never, ever alone.

And yet, I still feel lonely. Kellan hasn't contacted me since I told him I wasn't going to the walk. But to be fair, I haven't reached out to him either. It feels like there's a huge hole in my heart where he once was. And as much as I like spending time with Christina and her group, it's not the same. But I guess deep friendships take time to build, and I'm sure in time I'll feel that way about them too. Soon, hopefully.

I wake up way too early on Saturday morning. My body is buzzing, almost like it's in overdrive. It's too early to get dressed, so I try to distract myself by checking my e-mail. Besides a lot of spam, there's a message from the Muscular Dystrophy Society.

To: Molly Mahoney
From: Muscular Dystrophy Society
Subject: Good luck, Team Chocolate Chip Cookies!

Today's the big day! As a member of Kellan Bingham's team, here are some reminders for the day. Check-in starts at 9:00 a.m., and the Walk begins at 10:00. Parking is available in the municipal field parking lot, and volunteers will be on hand to help get you where you need to be. We hope you enjoy the day, and we thank you again for your support! People like you really do make a difference in the lives of those living with muscular dystrophy.

I sink into my desk chair and cover my face with my hands. I am not making a difference in the lives of those living with muscular dystrophy. I am not making a difference in the life of Kellan.

I am a terrible friend.

"Molly?" Eliza's knocking on my door, but before I can answer, she's standing inside my room.

"What's wrong with you?"

I slam my laptop shut and stand up. "Nothing. Why?"

"You don't look good."

"Thanks," I say.

Eliza shrugs. "Well, since it's my job to turn you into a glamour queen today, I have my work cut out for me. Come on. To the makeup mirror."

I follow her into her bedroom, and she has me sit down at her makeup table. She pulls out a big plastic case full of makeup, and I recognize it as the one I rummaged through when I was first creating my new look.

She pulls a small brush out of the case and dips it into some purple powder. "Close your eyes."

I do as I'm told, and the brush tickles as it travels over my eyelid. I giggle.

"Hold still," Eliza demands.

It takes her forever to finish, and when she does, I turn to look in the mirror.

"No!" she screams. "Not yet! You can't look until I do your hair."

Eliza moves on to my hair. She's twisting and turning and pulling it in all kinds of directions. I bite my lip so I don't say what I'm feeling, which is: *Owww!* I know she's doing me a favor, so I just squeeze my eyes shut whenever she yanks too hard.

"Okay." Eliza takes a step back. "Go put your dress on and then you can look in the mirror."

I speed-walk to my room, trying not to move the upper part of my body in case the vibration messes up my hair. I unbutton my pajamas, throw them on the bed, and slip into my dress first, followed by the sweater. I carry the shoes, since I don't want to have to wear them a minute longer than I have to.

Eliza's holding a silver necklace with matching earrings when I get back.

"Turn around," she says, and clasps the necklace behind me. She then hands me the earrings, which I put on myself.

"Now you can look." Eliza grabs my arm and pulls me toward her full-length mirror.

I stare at the person looking back at me, and I'm almost positive she isn't me.

First of all, I look at least five years older. My hair is in a French braid and pinned at the top, the different colors swirling together like a prism. The dye has faded by now, but the pastel tints that are left look even better next to the silver shrug. I look like a girl in a fashion magazine, with bright pink lips and black-lined eyes. And of course the dress completes the look. I look incredible. I look like a model. But I don't look like me.

"So, what do you think?" Eliza asks, tucking a loose hair back into its clip.

"It's amazing," I say. "How do you know how to do this?"

"I've been practicing on myself for years," she says. "Plus, I always do hair and makeup for my friends."

"You're really good at it," I say, still staring at the girl who is me but isn't me in the mirror.

Eliza grabs a pair of silver ballet flats out of her closet. "Throw these in your purse. They're soft and you can roll them up so they fit in there."

"But I already have shoes." I point to the high heels next to me.

"I know, but trust me, if there's any dancing or standing around, you'll want to wear these instead. They'll be much more comfortable. The heels are what you'll wear to make an entrance, but then you can switch to the flats once your feet hurt."

"There's so much I don't know." I sigh.

My phone beeps at the exact same time Eliza's does.

We both reach for them and then sit side by side on her bed. It's a text from Mom, to both of us.

I'm sorry for leaving the other night. I'd like to try again. Are you up for another family meeting?

I just stare at the text. Mom is apologizing? I'm not sure I remember that ever happening before.

Eliza throws her phone on her bed. "She's delusional if she thinks I'm going to go through that again."

"But she apologized," I say, still staring at the text in disbelief.

"So?" Eliza fixes her own lipstick in the mirror. "I haven't heard from her in over a week. And didn't you say she postponed your ice-cream date again last Tuesday? Too bad. It's too little too late."

I get why Eliza's upset, but I feel a glimmer of hope rise up inside of me like a firecracker in the sky—slow at first, then bursting wide open with light.

"We should give her a chance," I say.

Eliza caps her lipstick and throws it back into her makeup bag.

"Whatever," she says. "I have more important things to think about."

I take that as permission to text Mom back.

Okay. Let us know when.

Her response comes immediately.

I'll text your father to confirm the day and time.

Good. She's going to text Dad. That means they'll have to communicate. It's a good sign.

"All right!" Eliza shakes her head, like she's trying to get Mom out of her thoughts. "It's go time. You ready?"

I nod, and she follows me downstairs, where Dad is waiting with a camera. Coco tells me I look like an evil princess (because I'm wearing black and I have bright lipstick on), and Dad takes a few pictures.

My heart jumps inside my chest when the doorbell rings. I open it, and there stands Robert, in a black suit with a silver shirt and a black-and-silver-striped tie. But there's something else that makes him look so different than he usually does. His hair is gelled back. It's almost always flopping in his face.

"Wow!" Robert's eyes are wide. "You look awesome."

I'm glad I'm wearing so much makeup, because maybe he won't be able to tell I'm blushing. "So do you."

"You ready?" He points to the limo. "Everyone else is already inside."

I wave to Dad, Eliza, and Coco, and follow Robert into the limo. I've never been in a limo before, and when I open the door, I gasp. It looks like a living room on wheels! There are seats shaped like couches, a television, a mini fridge, and lighting across the very long ceiling. I slip in behind Robert, careful not to smoosh my dress.

"You look amazing," Nina says, and everyone else in the car echoes her, even Christina.

"Happy birthday," I say. "This is so great."

"You haven't seen anything yet," Christina says.

The limo backs out of our driveway, and the party begins.

chapter
* 28 *

THE ENTIRE LIMO RIDE IS SPENT TALKING ABOUT where everyone got their dresses. Christina got hers at Bloomingdale's. Taylor got hers at Nordstrom. Nina got hers at Macy's. And Devon and Izzy went shopping together at the designer boutiques in the outlet mall. When it's my turn, I tell everyone that I got this dress from my sister.

"Like, you mean, she bought it for you?" Christina asks.

"No," I say. "It used to be hers."

"Are you serious?" Christina tilts her head to the side. "You didn't even buy a new dress for the party?"

"Was I supposed to?" I whisper.

"No," Nina chimes in, her voice louder and stronger than usual. "Your dress is perfect."

"Yeah, it's fine for a hand-me-down," Christina adds,

giving Nina a nasty glare. She then turns around, presses the button to lower the divider, and talks to the driver. "Why are we slowing down?"

"There's a lot of traffic, miss," he says.

"Ugh. On a Saturday morning?" Christina says.

"There's a charity walk at the municipal field. That's what the holdup is."

"A walk? For what?"

"Um, the banner says muscular dystrophy," the driver answers.

"Well, that's stupid!" Christina turns around to face us now. "They're having a walk for people who can't actually walk!"

The entire limo busts out laughing. It's so loud that I flinch. I can't believe Christina said that. I can't believe everyone is laughing. Even Robert. But not Nina, I notice. She's looking down at her hands.

"Oh, good, we're moving again." Christina stretches her legs out. "We should be there any minute now. Can't you just smell the mochaccinos?"

The limo pulls up to the country club, and the driver comes around to open the door for us. And even though the sun feels good on my arms, I shiver, like I can't get warm enough.

Christina's parents meet us outside the front entrance

and usher us into a private room. This is the fanciest place I've ever been to. The chandeliers on the ceiling look like they're made of diamonds, and even the waiters and waitresses are dressed up. Our circular table is decorated with candles, shiny plates, and sparkling cups. In the center of the table is a bouquet of flowers that is bigger than the hedges in front of my house.

I sit between Robert and Nina, and the minute our butts hit the chairs, several waiters are at our table, pouring sparkling water, asking if we'd like anything else to drink, and making a huge fuss over everything we do. Soon other waiters and waitresses walk in with appetizers on trays, and before the meal is even served, our plates are loaded with food.

"That was a lot of traffic down the street," Christina's dad says.

"Yeah, it's a walk for some disease," Christina says. "But get this, it's a disease where the people who have it can't walk. So it's pretty ridiculous if you ask me."

My hands curl into fists. "Actually," I say, "it's a walk to raise money for muscular dystrophy."

"Whatever. Who cares?" Christina glares at me.

The blood pumps in my ears, and I stand up. "I care."

"What are you doing?" Robert whispers to me, but I ignore him.

"Muscular dystrophy is a serious disease. And the walk raises awareness and money for research so they can one day find a cure."

"Seriously?" Christina raises her voice. "Way to kill the mood."

"I just want you to understand that it's serious. And it's important." My voice is softer now.

"Well, it's not important to me, and it's my party, so let's all order mochaccinos!"

The table cheers, and I sit back down.

"What did you do that for?" Robert asks. "You're acting all crazy."

There's a tightness in my throat that's making it hard to breathe. Robert doesn't understand at all. "I can't stay here," I say.

"What?" Robert's voice has an edge I've never heard in it before. "The entire seventh grade would kill to be where you are right now."

"Maybe," I say. "But this isn't where I belong."

Robert rolls his eyes. "I give up."

"I need to get to Kellan's walk. That's where I should be right now."

"Kellan's walking?" Nina asks.

"Yes, and I signed up to be on his team, but then this party came up and I did this instead. But I shouldn't be here. I should be there. With him." Tears are burning my eyes, and I wipe them away with the back of my hand. I wonder if Eliza used waterproof makeup.

"I have to go tell Christina." I push my chair back and stand up. I walk to Christina's chair and bend down to talk to her.

"Christina, I'm really sorry," I whisper. "I appreciate that you invited me, but I have to go."

"Are you kidding me right now?" Her tone is sharp, and I can understand why.

"I'm sorry," I say again. "And I'll pay you for my food and everything."

"You're leaving?" Christina is yelling now, and the entire table stares at us.

"I have to. I promised a friend—"

"Oh. My. God," Christina says. "I can't even believe I invited you. You were a total loser before I took pity on you, and you're going to be a loser again. Go! I don't want any losers at the biggest party in town."

I stand up and stagger out of the room. I must look like such an idiot in my too-high heels that I can barely walk in, but I don't care. Beads of sweat sprout up on the back of my neck, and the sobs I've been trying to hold in come tumbling out. But I'm not crying about what

MOLLY IN THE MIDDLE

Christina said. I'm crying because I'm afraid I missed the most important day in Kellan's life.

I'm just heading to the lobby when I realize someone's following me.

"Molly!" Nina's running behind me, her purse dangling off of her shoulder.

"Nina, I'm so sorry I ruined the party," I say. "But I have to—"

"I know." Nina catches her breath. "You're going to find Kellan. I'm going with you."

"What?" My breath catches in my throat.

Nina nods. "I want to go with you. To the walk. I've always liked Kellan, and when I heard Christina talk like that, well . . ." Her voice trails off. "Do you even know how to get to where the walk is?"

"Yeah, it's right down the road," I say. "But it started at ten o'clock."

Nina pulls her phone out of her purse. "It's ten fifteen. Maybe we can still catch him."

We both run out the door, kick off our shoes, and take off as fast as we possibly can toward the municipal field.

chapter
* 29 *

OUR FEET ARE SOAKED FROM RUNNING THROUGH THE
wet grass. Nina slips her shoes back on (her heels aren't
nearly as high as mine), and I put on the ballet flats that
Eliza gave me.

"This place is packed," Nina says.

Hundreds and hundreds of people have already started
walking, everybody in blue Muscular Dystrophy Society
shirts or team shirts, like the ones Kellan and I made. I
don't know how we'll possibly find him in this crowd.

"Follow me," I say to Nina as I make my way to the
edge of the pack. They'll be walking, but we'll be running.
Hopefully, that will allow us to get a glimpse of the walkers
and eventually find Kellan.

Many of the participants give us confused looks as

we run by. We're definitely overdressed. My dress is sticking to my back, and my hair is falling out of its French braid. When I rub the sweat out of my eye, my hand comes back black. I can only imagine what my face must look like. Nina, on the other hand, is grace under pressure. Her hair hasn't moved, and her lipstick is still perfect. Maybe she's had more practice getting dressed up than I have.

We're almost at the middle of the pack when I spot Kellan. He's with his mom, his dad, and Dylan, who are all decked out in Team Chocolate Chip Cookies shirts.

"Kellan!" I scream, but between the music that's blaring from nearby speakers and all the people talking, he doesn't hear me.

"Kellan!" I yell again, and Nina and I sprint to catch up with him.

He does a double take when he sees us. And then he stops walking. He whispers something to his mom, who whispers back to him.

Oh no. Mrs. Bingham knows. She knows what a terrible person I am. I feel like I shrink at least a foot as Nina and I make our way over to them.

"What are you guys doing here?" Kellan is standing with his arms crossed, with his parents on one side of him and Dylan on the other.

"We've come to walk." I hope and pray that he can forgive me. I cross my fingers for extra luck.

"Sorry." Kellan turns away from me. "Dylan took your place."

I look at Dylan wearing the T-shirt I designed for us, and I feel a twinge of jealousy.

It never occurred to me—until right this very second—that maybe while I was replacing Kellan as my best friend, he was replacing me as well.

"I'm sorry," I blurt out. "I don't blame you for being mad."

Mrs. Bingham puts her hand on Kellan's shoulder. "How about if we meet you up ahead?"

Kellan nods, and Mr. and Mrs. Bingham continue walking with the crowd. Dylan looks confused, like he doesn't know where to go, so he just stays put.

Kellan still doesn't say anything to me, which means he may be willing to listen. I take this as an invitation to keep going.

"I've been a terrible friend."

Kellan snorts.

"The worst friend ever," I continue. "I know. I see that now. I'm sorry it took me so long to really figure it out. But you are my best friend, Kellan. And there's nowhere I'd rather be right now than here. So even if you kick me off of Team Chocolate Chip Cookies, I'm still walking."

"You know, Molly," Kellan says softly, "you were the only person I truly trusted, and when you bailed on me . . ."

"I know." My eyes fill with tears. "I know, and I'm so sorry. I—"

"No." Kellan puts his hand up. "Let me finish. I needed you. But maybe that was the problem. I hid behind you, and I hid behind this stupid disease of mine. I used both of you to justify to myself that I was fine. But you know what? I wasn't fine. I'm not fine."

Kellan adjusts his weight from one leg brace to the other and keeps talking. "I got a raw deal. And maybe you got a raw deal too. You wanted to be more special, and I wanted to be less special."

The tears that filled my eyes a few minutes ago are now pouring down my cheeks. I want to hug him and apologize again and again, but he's still talking.

"We are who we are, I guess. When I stopped talking to you, I started talking to my mom. I mean *really* talking. And I learned how to talk to other kids too. I even met a few today with muscular dystrophy, just like me. That's something I never would have done if you had been here with me. So it occurred to me—maybe that's why you made other friends at school: because I wasn't there with you. Maybe you weren't only my crutch, but I was yours too."

Now I'm full-out ugly crying. Even waterproof mascara doesn't stand a chance against the deluge of tears gushing out of my eyes. The truth is, he's right. It was always the two of us, until all of a sudden it wasn't. And when we no longer had each other, we had to find others to lean on—or maybe we had to learn to lean on ourselves.

"I love you, Kels," I manage to say between heavy sobs. "I just want us to be friends again. Things don't have to be like they used to be. They can be even better. I mean, Dylan's here. And Dylan's great. And Nina's here too. And she's great. Can't we be friends with them but also best friends with each other?"

Nina and Dylan give each other shy smiles, but Kellan doesn't say a word. He just looks at me, his eyes blank.

And then, after an excruciating silence, Kellan cracks up. He laughs until he's doubled over.

"What's so funny?" Did I just pour out my heart to have him stomp all over it?

"Have you looked at yourself?" Kellan says in between fits of laughter. "You're a mess."

"It's been a long morning," I say.

"What happened to the party?"

Nina and I look at each other. "We left," she says.

"You left the party?" Kellan asks. "Like, in the middle of it?"

"Just as it was starting," I say, wiping my eyes. "We knew there was someplace else we'd rather be."

Kellan's face turns pink. "Well, if you're going to walk, you'll need to wear the team uniform." Kellan reaches into his backpack and pulls out two T-shirts.

"These are adorbs!" Nina squeals as Kellan hands her one.

"Molly designed them," Kellan says.

"With pride," I say as I pull the shirt on over my dress. Nina does the same thing, then the four of us join the pack of walkers headed forward on the route.

"So we're okay?" I ask Kellan as I try to wipe eyeliner off my cheeks.

"We're okay," he says with a grin.

"It was really nice of you to come with me," I say to Nina.

"I wanted to," she says. "Kellan's a better friend than Christina will ever be."

"You know," I say, shaking my head, "I was so worried that Christina wouldn't like me that I never bothered to ask myself if I liked her."

"I know that feeling," Nina says.

"And this morning the answer slapped me in the face," I tell her.

"I think we'll be better off without her," Nina says with a chuckle. "We'll just have to find a new lunch table."

"You can sit at our table," Dylan offers.

"Yeah!" Kellan loops one arm in mine and the other arm in Nina's, who then loops her arm in Dylan's, until we form a human chain. We're not going fast, but supporting one another, we know we're going to make it.

Sure enough, a few miles later, with the sun directly overhead, the finish line comes in sight.

"Hey!" I say to Kellan. "Look! You did it!"

"We did it," he corrects me. "Team Chocolate Chip Cookies!"

We cross the finish line arm in arm. A photographer is waiting to take our picture. He has a quizzical look on his face, probably wondering why I have a walk T-shirt over semiformal wear and why I have smeared makeup all over my face, but I don't care how ridiculous I look. I'm thrilled that Kellan crossed the finish line. And I'm thrilled that I was by his side when he did. And now I want life to go back to normal, when the only people who knew my name were the only people who really matter.

Acknowledgments

Thank you to everyone at Simon & Schuster who helped bring Molly to life, especially my wonderful editor, Alyson Heller. It's a joy to work with you!

Much gratitude to my agent, the amazing Sarah Davies, for your hard work and brilliant insight.

As always, big love to the MGBetaReaders, the best critique group in the whole wide world. Special thanks to Molly's early readers: Dana Edwards, Laurie Litwin, and Gail Nall.

Thank you to the Camden Public Library in Camden, Maine, for providing the most inspiring and gorgeous place to write, and especially the one and only Amy Hand, for your support and friendship. All librarians are special, but you are truly a shining star.

I'm grateful for the community I have found with my friends at Watershed School and at Ashwood Waldorf School. We got so lucky when we landed here in Midcoast Maine with all of you welcoming and wonderful people.

Thank you to Hallie, Morgan, Josh, and my parents for being my first readers—and my biggest supporters. My love for you is immeasurable.

And finally, huge thanks to you, the reader, for choosing to spend your time with Molly and friends.

Turn the page for a look at another great read from Ronni Arno.

MY BROTHER IS SMILING SO HARD I THINK HIS CHEEKS
are pinned to his ears. This would be fine, of course, if we
weren't at my grandfather's funeral.

I elbow him in the ribs.

"What was that for?" He rubs his side.

"You shouldn't look so happy at a funeral," I hiss.

"I'm not *happy*," he says. "I'm just glad Grandad's in
a better place."

"And that his truck is still here," I say, teeth clenched.

"Grandad loved that truck, and he wanted me to have
it," Troy whispers. "And it's not like he ever drove it once
he went into the nursing home."

"It doesn't matter." I cross my arms. "He's dead
and it's sad."

My father turns around in the pew in front of us and puts his finger to his lips. "Shhhhh."

I point at Troy with my thumb to show my dad that it was clearly his fault. My dad just shakes his head and turns back around in his seat.

The minister is droning on about how Grandad is reunited with Grandmom and Mom. My stomach sinks a little when I hear Mom's name. I hope and pray that she's up there somewhere, hanging out with her parents, playing Scrabble, looking down on us and smiling. But I don't know. I've asked for a sign every single day since she died five years ago, and I've gotten nothing. Not even one little boo. It's hard to believe that her spirit is still around but never bothered to get in touch.

Finally, we file out of the church. Dad shakes hands with some guy I don't recognize. Like most everyone else in this town, he has a white beard and long white hair—a skinny Santa Claus. Dad looks uncomfortable, shifting from foot to foot, hands fiddling around with his tie. I know he wants to get out of here as soon as possible, but I can't tell if it's because of Skinny Santa Claus, or because he hasn't stepped foot near a church since Mom died.

After the service we follow the hearse to the cemetery. The gray, rainy day makes it look even creepier than it already is. By the time we get to Grandad's grave, I feel like I swallowed a tombstone. We pull up to Grandad's new home—a hole in the ground. At least he's got good neighbors. Grandmom's grave is next to his, and next to hers is Mom's. I haven't been here in a couple of years. Maybe that's why Mom's spirit doesn't visit. She's mad at me for ditching her.

When the casket is ready to go into the ground, Dad squeezes my hand. He looks like he just ate a lemon covered in hot sauce. His eyes keep wandering over to Mom's grave.

DAPHNE PICKLER
DEVOTED WIFE AND MOTHER
APRIL 3, 1973–MARCH 21, 2011

Her grave site is totally bare. No flowers, no teddy bears, no nothing. I kick myself for not bringing something along with me. Duh. Why didn't I realize that Grandad would be buried with Mom? If Mom wasn't mad before, I'm sure she's furious by now.

I pull my hand out of Dad's and stuff it in my pocket. *He* was supposed to be the one to bring something for Mom. *He* was supposed to know that we were going to be here. *He* was supposed to be the grown-up.

Except that he isn't and he hasn't been. Not since Mom died.

They put Grandad in the ground. I know Troy is right and Grandad hasn't been Grandad for years, but my eyes don't realize this, and tears leak out of them. I quickly wipe them away with the back of my hand. I glance up at Dad, who has his head down and his lips pursed. I feel a twinge of pity for him. Grandad wasn't his father, but he never knew his own father and Grandad was the closest thing he had. Poor Dad, he—

I give myself a mental slap. I am *not* giving Dad a ride on the pity train.

The service ends, and we walk back to the car.

"Can I drive?" Troy eagerly holds out his hands for the keys.

"Not a chance," I pipe in. "I'm not driving with him."

"I have my permit," Troy says. "And anyway, who do you think is going to drive you around when we move?"

What?

"Troy!" Dad shakes his head.

"Oops." Troy slinks to the passenger-side door.

"We're moving?" I ask, after I pick my jaw up off the ground.

Dad turns to look at me. He tries to take my hand again, but I cross my arms instead.

"Poppy, honey." Dad takes a deep breath. "We've moved from tiny apartment to tiny apartment over the last few years. Things haven't exactly been stable."

I snort at the understatement.

"That was your mom's biggest complaint. She always said we needed to go somewhere we could have roots."

I can't believe Dad's trying to use Mom to talk me into this. He hasn't talked about Mom in years.

"Your grandad left us the house." His voice takes on a giddy tone, as if this is the best news ever. "And I think we should move into it and start our lives over. And the house is paid for, so I won't have to be out working so much. We could spend more time together. We could have a real home."

"But here? In a haunted house on hillbilly hill? What about school? What about my friends?"

"The house isn't haunted, Poppy. And don't call the locals hillbillies. Your mom grew up here, you know."

I feel a twinge of guilt pull at my stomach. I didn't mean *Mom* was a hillbilly.

"And you can still see your friends. We can visit each summer." Dad smiles as if I should be doing backflips at the news of seeing my friends once a year.

Ugh. I happen to know for a fact that the house is haunted. Grandmom used to tell me all the time. I know she tried to make it not-scary by saying that the ghosts were friendly, like Casper, but let's face it: How many friendly cartoon ghosts are there in the real world? And based on the people at Grandad's funeral, this place *is* the hillbilly hub of the world.

"And what if I say no?" I cross my arms with finality.

"I'm sorry." Dad sighs. "But the decision's been made. We're going to go over there now and check things out, and then we'll move our things in over the weekend."

I wait for him to say more, but he doesn't. I open my mouth to scream and yell and demand to know why he's all of a sudden deciding to become a parent when he's been nearly absent for the last five years. But instead of words coming out, I just sob. I turn my back on him, open the door, and crawl into the backseat. How can he expect me to switch schools now, in the middle of seventh grade? Isn't there some kind of cruelty-to-children law about that?

But my mouth won't work, except to leak out ugly gurgling sounds. My dad keeps looking at me in the rearview mirror, but I'm pretty sure his brain turns off at the sound of crying.

My grandparents' old farmhouse sits off a country road, which is miles away from any town center, mall, restaurant, or actual people. Our closest neighbors are a flock of sheep and a herd of cattle. I used to love visiting when I was little. Grandad would always help me pick berries, and let me sit on his lap while he drove the tractor up and down the fields. I was seven the last time I was at the farmhouse. I remember because it was a few months before Mom died and Grandad went into the nursing home. Yep, that was a stellar year.

Dad parks the car next to the garage. Everything looks exactly the same. Grandad had a caretaker living here before he died. But I guess the place is ours now.

The house looks just like I remember it. A giant porch wraps around the building, and the forest-green rocking chairs are in the exact same place they've always been. Mom used to sit me on her lap for hours and we'd rock back and forth, drinking lemonade with fresh mint leaves dropped in. Mom loved mint, and every time I smell it I think of her.

I swallow hard. This place is full of Mom memories, and they come flooding back to me with every whiff of hay and every step in the freshly mowed green grass.

"There she is!" Troy leaps over to Grandad's pickup truck, parked next to the barn. He taps the door gently. "How are you doing, baby? Ready for a new life?"

I roll my eyes. How can Troy be happy about this? Is getting a truck better than switching schools in the middle of the year? Better than leaving the city we've called home since birth? Then I remember how easily Troy can be bought—and distracted. When Mom died, Dad got him a puppy. But Troy got sick of taking care of it after a few months, and we gave it to my cousins who lived in the suburbs. So Dad got him an Xbox instead, and he seemed perfectly content with that.

While Dad and Troy *oooooh* and *aaaaaah* over the truck, I wander over to the barn. Troy and I played hide-and-seek when we were younger, and there was no better hiding spot than the hay bales in the loft. I slide open the barn door, and the memories practically push me over—or maybe it's the stench of horse poop.

The stalls are empty now, but it still smells exactly the same. I climb up the ladder to the loft. The hay bales are still here. I squeeze myself in between two of them and sit there, breathing in the familiar smell of straw. Maybe if I hide in here long enough, I'll be able to miss the rest of seventh grade altogether.

This was a great hiding spot when I was seven, but not so great now that I'm twelve. There's not enough room in between the bales, so I wriggle my butt until each hay bale slides away, giving me more room to sit. I scooch backward until I realize I'm sitting on something hard and pointy.

I quickly stand up and spot the edge of wallboard sticking out. One of the panels must have come loose and fallen down into the hay. I reach my hand out to close it, when I notice a metal box crammed inside. I squeeze my hand into the crack and pull out the box. It's silver, and about the size of a textbook. When I lift it up, I can tell that something's sliding around inside. There's no lock, but it won't open. I pry my fingernails under the lid and pull. The lid pops off, flies through the air, and lands with a *clank* on the barn floor.

Inside are letters. A whole stack of letters, tied up in a rubber band. I flip through the envelopes and notice they all have the same name neatly printed on the outside.

Poppy.

These letters are to me.

I stare at my name. Did someone know we were coming? But why would they leave the letters here, hidden in a stack of hay? And why do they look so *old*?

There are numbers at the top of each envelope. I pull the envelope labeled *#1* out of the rubber band holding the stack together, and flip it over. It's sealed.

Do I open it?

I have to open it. It's not like I'm spying or breaking some sort of federal mail law, or even invading someone's privacy. The letters are addressed to me.

Before I can change my mind, I rip open the top of the yellowed envelope.